Charity's Choice

Alexine Crawford

Charity's Choice

Published by The Conrad Press in the United Kingdom 2019

Tel: +44(0)1227 472 874
www.theconradpress.com
info@theconradpress.com

ISBN 978-1-911546-64-1

Typesetting and Cover Design by:
Charlotte Mouncey, www.bookstyle.co.uk

The Conrad Press logo was designed by Maria Priestley.

Printed and bound in Great Britain
by Clays Ltd, Elcograf S.p.A.

Who is who and Locations

FARNHAM

The Mannory Family
James, tannery foreman
Thomas, carter
Jacob and Phoebe, their
parents
Abigail, sister, married to
Ralph Attfield
Hal, their adopted son.

Charity
Ned and Margie, her sister
and brother-in-law

The Gary Family
Michael, woollen draper
Betty his wife
Ann their daughter
Christopher, Robert, Mike,
Nathaniel, George, Eliza,
Jane, their other children
Abe Trussler, rival tanner
and carter
Wroth, town Bailiff and
linen draper
Vernon, gentleman, of
Culver House

LONDON
William Kiffin, merchant
and Baptist
Hanna his wife
Lydia their daughter.
Lambe and Patience,
Baptist pastors

Campaigners for justice
John Lilburne married to
Elizabeth
Richard Overton married
to Mary
John Wildman, 'the
soldiers' mouth'

The Army
Fairfax,
Commander-in-Chief
Cromwell, General.
Sir William Waller,
ex-General
Jim Hosier, ex-soldier,
ex-coachman

From America
John Woodbridge
Walter Hutchcroft

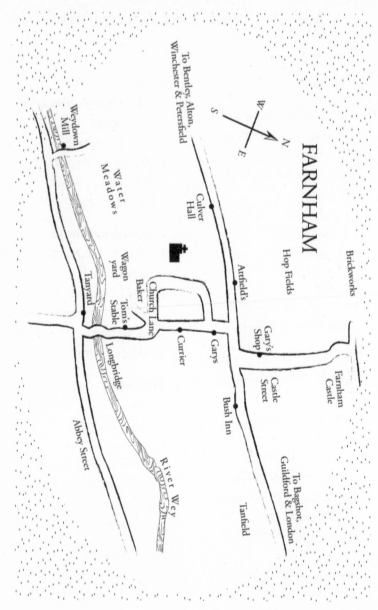

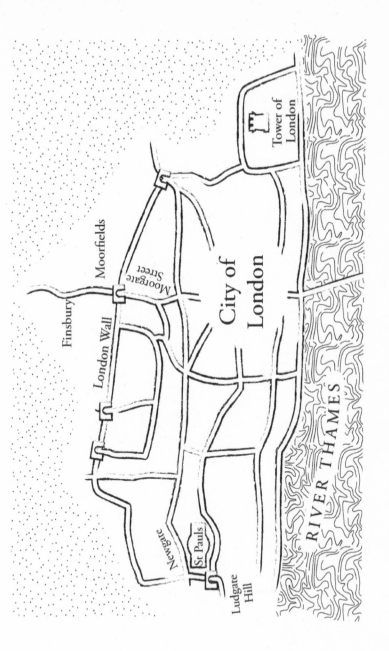

Finsbury

Moorfields

Moorgate Street

London Wall

Newgate

St Pauls

Ludgate Hill

City of London

Tower of London

RIVER THAMES

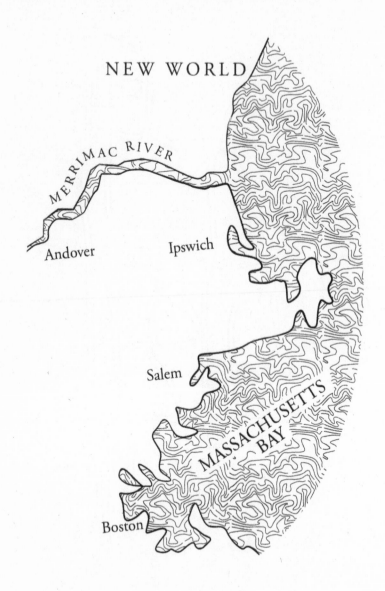

NEW WORLD

MERRIMAC RIVER

Andover

Ipswich

Salem

MASSACHUSETTS
BAY

Boston

1632

Martha ran through the farm kitchen and out to the yard crying 'Walter!' too fast to hear her mother's habitual 'That man!' She was out, pulling Walter off his horse, smothering him with kisses.

'Congratulate me!' he said. 'It's all arranged!'

Momentarily she pulled back from him. 'We're to go?'

'Not you, my sweetheart.' He put his arm around her and drew her towards the farm house. Her formidable mother almost barred the way in. 'Well?' she said. Her husband hesitated behind her.

'Indentured servant,' Walter said. 'He pays the passage, I serve him for a few years, and after that who knows what will come my way!'

'Work for who? Where?' breathlessly.

'My friend, the Vicar's son, got employment there already.'

'But where?'

'Why, the New World. I told you. Massachusetts. Over the ocean.'

Suddenly the room was filled with silence. The farmer broke the silence. 'You're taking my daughter over that dreadful sea?' he asked.

'No no, I'll not take her at first. Not with child. A pioneering life. Settlers have died. No, I'll send for her later on.'

'So what is so special about Massachusetts?'

'Freedom!' Walter flung out his arms. 'Laws they make for themselves, no dominating church, think what you will, say what you like. Freedom!'

'You always say and do what you like.' His mother-in-law's tone was bitter. 'And she's the same, her nose into everything. Indentured servant indeed! You're not one to serve anyone.'

'I'm not afraid of work,' Walter protested. 'I'm to be his general factotum. It's all arranged. I'm off to Southampton tomorrow to await the ship.'

Chapter 1 - 1647: The Mannory Brothers

James Mannory burst into Tanyard House, slamming the yard door, anger vibrating every muscle in his body. The door swung noisily, the latches clattering. He was too angry to bother to close it. He paced up and down the long hall, the whole ground floor of the house, yet scarcely large enough to contain his pacing, his fury. If anyone had crossed his path he would have hit them, so consumed was he with anger.

Beating that stupid apprentice had in no way relieved his frustrations. He had beaten him soundly, ignoring his cries, and left the men to clear up at the day's end.

Now pacing around the long table and benches, he was too angry to be able to think, too angry to begin to see why the apprentice's ineptitude with rounding a hide – and not his first attempt – had so aroused his temper. The knife in the lad's hand had wobbled and strayed as he tried to cut the big skin to shape, damaging yet another hide. And James' impatience had exploded into fury.

The garden door latch clicked, quietly. Tanyard House, set at right-angles to the River Wey, had the door from the yard that James had used and another, the opposite side of the big central chimney, leading to the garden. The apprentices had avoided him by going round the river end of the house, to the garden door. That gave access to the stairway, winding up two storeys. The stair creaked as they crept up to the loft where they slept.

James flopped into his father Jacob's high backed chair, beside the hearth with its pile of cold ash.

No one but Jacob sat in this chair. No one but Jacob was boss of the tannery. Four years now James had been foreman, but still his father controlled, checked, kept the ledgers, refused change.

Had he, James, made all the wrong choices? That stupid lad was just the peak of his discontent. Back when war broke out between King Charles and his Parliament, James, an enthusiastic militiaman, thought reforms might come of it. But King Charles' belief in his divine right as King never wavered and he fought to secure his personal rule. Loyalties were split across the nation, and no battle was final. Disillusioned, James opted out and returned to the family tannery. Despite later victories won by the more professional New Model Army, making King Charles a prisoner, pockets of Royalist resistance remained. Nothing was settled. The fight had been against King Charles' arbitrary government, yet the victors were almost as arbitrary, guarding their own interests. Parliament was fragmenting into rival groups, each struggling for power, while James' own struggles amounted to no more than daily frustration with his father Jacob.

Outside in the yard the mastiffs, chained inside the gate from the lane, barked as it was opened, and a cart rumbled into the yard. 'Thomas Mannory, Carrier' the sides of the cart proclaimed. Mild contented brother Thomas, he was somehow a threat in himself. He was building up his own business, with his own horses and carts. He was independent except for stabling, and that he still lived in Tanyard House. Not that carting had the same prestige as the skilled tanning trade.

James put his head in his hands, nothing resolved.

He was still there when Thomas breezed in smelling of horse, his carter's smock open at the neck because the day was hot.

'Hullo,' he said, 'Down in the dumps?' Then, 'Lord, you'll catch it sitting in Father's chair.'

'We're not children. He's not the King.' Nonetheless James got up.

'What's up with you then? Such a beautiful day.'

'Nothing you'd grasp.'

'Oh oh!'

James gave him a withering look.

'What you need,' Thomas said cheerfully, 'is a wife.'

'I do, do I.' James barely muttered.

'Look how Mother soothes Father.'

'I don't need soothing!'

'What is it you do want?'

'Nothing you'd understand. Just leave me be.'

'You need a wife.' Thomas knew he was being provocative. 'What about one of the Gary girls? Three to choose from with all those brothers, how would that be?'

'Oh go away!' James shouted, thumping the table with his fist. 'You know nothing at all!'

It was early May, when work started at dawn and they ate at midday. Now the fire was cold. The apprentices and resident journeymen would soon be round the table for their evening bite to eat. He could not bear to sit with them over bread and ale, and his father's nightly Bible reading. He would go across bridge and meadow to the Bush and drink alone. At least now that the war had dwindled to an end the inns were not swarming with billeted troops.

15

The cheerful crowd in the Bush jarred, so he scarcely finished his beaker of ale before heading back home. A late wagon constricted the long bridge over the River Wey. He chafed waiting for it to move. He kicked at the mastiffs greeting him just inside the yard. He went round to the garden door and stormed up the stairs to the bedroom he shared with Thomas.

There he pulled out a box from under the bed. At least he could read the latest pamphlets, learn of reformers' struggles in London, yearn for democracy. In recent years an explosion of printing and publishing had opened up opinions to the many who could read. Most publications were illegal because they were not licensed by the monopoly Stationers Company, but they spread widely nonetheless, seemingly unstoppable.

He had scarcely started when Thomas came in from his evening in the Goat's Head, infuriatingly cheerful.

'Is that the latest newsbook?' he asked.

James growled.

'Looks a bit fat for a newsbook,' Thomas said.

James held it up.

'*The oppressed man's oppressions declared*', Thomas read. 'Are you oppressed, brother James?' He laughed.

'You do not have the slightest idea what is happening,' James said. 'So long as that cart of yours can move stuff from place to place, you don't care what goes on in the rest of the world.'

'What if I did, there's not much you seem able to do about it.'

There was the rub, and Thomas had hit right on it. James flung the pamphlets back in the box, slammed the lid shut, and said, 'I'm going to bed.'

'Think how nice that would be,' Thomas could not resist a final prod, 'if you had a wife to go there with.'

Jacob Mannory's office was perched up a steep stair in the corner of the tannery yard, opposite Tanyard house. From it he could look down on the series of pits where hides hung suspended in the tanning liquor. To his left the yard sloped down to the river Wey, and the lime pits which began the tanning process.

To his right he could see into the open sided fleshing sheds, above which louvred windows concealed the drying sheds. His domain and no less his responsibility. Tall, slim and upright, unlike his stockier elder son James, Jacob wore his sixty years well, almost as agile as his sons.

He readily admitted that it was his wife Phoebe who kept her finger on the pulse of family and household, discerning what was going on. But whether he was up at his ledgers or down among the men, in the tannery he missed nothing. And now as a highly respected tanner he had an unwelcome role to play.

Today was market day. He waited impatiently for James to come up with the list of hides to take to market. He still chafed at leaving their selection to James.

Drinking at the Bush had done little to cool down James. Soon after work began he checked through the hides hanging in the drying shed, selected those ready for sale and told the men to load them on the hand cart. He went up to the office.

'About time!' Jacob said. 'I see they're loaded. Have you checked them?'

'Of course they're checked!' James said, 'and on the hand cart.'

They went down to the yard together. 'What is in that sack?' Jacob asked.

'Fine skins,' James said. 'We've had a good number come in lately.'

'Rabbit!' Jacob said scornfully.

'Not only rabbit. Lambskins too, and even some kid. I'd like to be selling to London. The Leathersellers in the City want good skins at a good price. My friend William Kiffin in London...'

'Enough of that,' Jacob said. 'I have to be at the Bailiffs' Hall very shortly.' As they walked, James raised a questioning eyebrow.

'Abe Trussler again,' Jacob said.

James sighed. 'We've not had much trouble with him for a while. What's he been up to this time?'

'He's been heading this way for a while,' Jacob said, 'hides not up to standard. On last market day the Under Bailiff refused to stamp some of the hides he brought in for sale.'

James whistled. 'Has anything like that happened before?'

Jacob ignored the question.

'I've been called to make up the six jurors to assess them. If we agree, Trussler will be fined and he'll forfeit the defective hides.'

'That will fuel up the old feud,' James said.

'There's no feud,' Jacob said firmly. 'A feud needs two parties and I have never feuded with Trussler.'

Without altering his pace he said, 'That was a severe beating I heard last evening.'

James flared. 'I was reared to beatings.'

'I cannot deny that I have been ready with the rod. You are perhaps too ready. And now...'

'If you're talking about that fool apprentice, it was justified. He damages hides.'

'Let him practise with the knives on a hide he has damaged.'

'He won't learn.'

Jacob looked up. 'Is he afraid of you?'

For a moment they paused and held each other's gaze. That from Jacob! His children had all been afraid of him, and of his control. And he was still controlling James.

Fear transferred itself, so of course the lad was afraid of James, even more so when temper had overtaken anger and he had beaten him long and hard.

Jacob joined the other jurors upstairs in the Bailiffs' Hall, which stood almost opposite the Bush Inn.

The Under Bailiff had laid out the offending hides in a low pile, which occupied a quarter of the floor space. To a casual glance the hides seemed to be in order. They were stiff, rigid, the size of a cow's back, not yet softened and oiled by a currier to make them usable as leather. Jacob lifted the corner of one and felt it.

'Spongey,' he said, 'And the colour's not right.'

A fellow juror came up beside him.

'Reckon he's gone for speed,' he said.

Jacob nodded. 'The tannin hasn't had time to penetrate properly. Or maybe he's tried hot water and ash at some stage.'

They moved the hide to inspect the two in the pile below. All bore similar evidence of defective tanning. None could be stamped for sale – reputations hung on this.

Abe Trussler had been told to wait down the stairs, and now they called him up. He had not bothered to tidy himself. His hair stuck out in greasy strands from under his work-stained cap, and the shirt under his breeches and jerkin was a stranger to soap.

George Wroth, one of the Town's two Bailiffs spoke. 'These are your hides?'

Abe grunted with a reluctant nod.

'We have conferred, and we agree with the Under Bailiff that they cannot be stamped for sale. Have you anything to say?'

Abe looked from face to face, men most of whom knew tanning, but men who might have a grudge against him. And Jacob Mannory among them. Mistrust flickered around his mouth, but he said nothing.

'The hides of course are forfeit,' Wroth said, 'and the recognised fine is ten shillings.'

At this Abe exploded. 'Ten blinking shillings! I ain't got ten shillings. My cart's broke, badly mended by some fool, the horse is lame. Ten shillings! You have it in for me, you self-righteous citizens! I'll not pay it. I will not pay it.'

The jurors glanced at one another.

'Mannory!' Abe said. 'It would be you. So much for your Christian virtue! Father of a bastard, son of a mean tanner ...' and he spat.

'That is not relevant,' Wroth said. 'You have until next Market day to pay the fine, and these hides are forfeit.'

By Sunday James had simmered down.

Jacob Mannory insisted on everyone in his household attending church, obeying the law. It was all automatic as far as James was concerned. He could remember as a child enjoying the services, because of the singing. Hearty singing with new songs and metrical psalms raised the roof. He didn't bother much with the readings and prayers, much the same every week.

Then when he was fifteen came the new bishop who wanted to change everything. The table which had stood centrally in the body of the church was moved far up the steps to the distant east end. No longer did they gather like a family around the table. The rite became almost popish, with the Rector or his dandy Curate right up in front and the table now an altar. They were expected to kneel in front of it, not passing loaf and chalice of wine from hand to hand, but receiving it in bits and sips from the priest with all his bowing and bobbing up and down.

The Town Burgesses refused to spend out on altar rails, so some people stood and some knelt on the cold stone step. Nor would the Burgesses allow this Bishop to abolish preaching, but continued to pay for a lecture on Market days.

Then the Rector had been accused of adultery and fled with his curate to Oxford. The lecturer became Rector in his place. He returned the table, altar no more, to its former position.

For James, church was a duty, and what did all these alterations and disputes matter? A piece of furniture, whatever you called it, a bodily posture, a surplice covering the Rector's everyday clothes, none held significance for him. Religious controversies masked the real, the important issues, of justice and fairness and the freedom they had been fighting for.

But today, unusually, his attention was caught. The Rector was reading out of the book of Proverbs. The chapters seemed to be just a list, a list indeed of proverbs. He paused after each proverb, and suddenly one impacted James.

'A brother's help is like a strong city, but quarrelling is like the bars of a castle.'

Brother! he thought. Some help he is, provoking with a smile, particularly in their shared bedroom. Yet never actually quarrelling.

And then a few proverbs later came, 'He who finds a wife finds a good thing, and obtains favour from the Lord.'

He stopped listening.

Some people claimed that God spoke to them, though he never took that seriously. Too many on opposing sides in the recent war claimed to be guided by God. Yet there was something odd about these three things coming together - Thomas saying he needed a wife, the bit about a brother and now this proverb that finding a wife would be a blessing.

Would a wife fit into his life, or try to control it? Would a wife have the least understanding of his trade, of the heavy physical demands of tanning, the chemical skills, or of the national issues that so desperately concerned him? How would he know who would be a blessing as a wife? Someone who cooked well and kept a clean and orderly house, like his mother Phoebe? Better than the young maids Phoebe always seemed to be training.

The reading over, singing began again. As he sang he looked across the table where it happened that the Gary family was lined up. He had never really looked at them before. The parents of course he knew, Michael the woollen draper and Betty the gossip, and he had known Christopher from school days. However, he had never bothered to consider the rest of that numerous family.

Now he looked at them, five boys of varying ages besides Christopher, and three girls, neatly and identically dressed, the smallest girl a young child. The girls looked remarkably alike, with an inherited prettiness that in their mother had been overtaken by child-bearing. Good breeding stock he found himself thinking, and then felt a little ashamed at the thought.

When the service concluded he made a point of greeting Michael Gary. 'Is all well with Christopher?' he asked.

'Aye, but he begged to be excused today.'

Betty Gary was quickly beside him. 'His wife Joan is so near her time you know, and she's that nervous about the delivery, you'd think no one had birthed a child before. Now Ann!' she turned to her eldest daughter, 'don't let the children out of your sight!' She turned back to James. 'It's a sheep dog I need when they're all together.'

'And Ann is your sheep dog?'

'She can be, but she needs reminding. The little boys are such a handful, if it's not one it's another, or all three up to some mischief. Ann! Where is Nathanael? George! That is not for climbing! Forgive me, they need to run about outside.'

She herded them with her hands through the door, Ann bringing up the rear.

'Your mother must be grateful for your help,' he ventured to say to her. She raised an eyebrow at him but said nothing.

Often on a Sunday afternoon James would go upstairs to the bedroom he shared with Thomas, and read the latest news books and any pamphlets he had managed to buy.

Today, the day was too sparkling fine to be spent indoors with the light of just one small window. He crossed the bridge and set off eastward along the River Wey through the meadows which stretched on and on. The grass was lush and full of flowers, white ladies' bedstraw, golden-headed dandelions and buttercups, with willows trailing their delicate fronds in the gentle breeze.

Odd about this morning, he found himself thinking. Odd that the idea of a wife should suddenly come up. He thought around it as he walked. To be in his own house, making his own plans, perhaps even released a bit from his father. Not to share a room with his brother – but then he would be sharing with a wife. That could mean less freedom, less privacy.

A well-established family, the Garys. Christopher a woollen draper with his father and already married to a well-dowried wife. But supposing the daughter Ann was like her mother, a gossip with her nose into everything, a nose that was sometimes spiteful. She probably had not enough education to be bothered with his own concerns. You did not expect this in a maiden anyway, and she might not even be able to read and write.

Approaching a bend in the river he realised he was passing Abe Trussler's place, a small collection of sheds and an unkempt yard. There was no gate and he paused in the lane to look in. Like in their own tanyard, Abe had pits aligned down to the river, but not all of them looked to be in use. The sheds leant as if some vital support had rotted. The cart, abandoned just inside the yard, was indeed broken.

Suddenly Abe himself emerged from his cottage.

'Another Mannory!' he shouted. 'Spying, are you? Spying for father!'

James shook his head. 'Just happened to be passing. No need to shout at me!'

'You can mind your own business, that's what you can do,' still shouting. 'If it's not one Mannory it's another,' and then a cough temporarily silenced him. When he regained his breath he croaked, 'Get out of here!'

Confound the man! James thought as he turned away, the pleasure of the afternoon overshadowed. He felt irritation rising. His role in the tannery, his father's rule, this business with Abe Trussler's hides, his own powerlessness in the epic struggle for justice and freedom he could only read about, tangled around in his head, each as insoluble as the other. No wonder anger sometimes took over with all this frustration burning him up.

'What you need...,' a faint echo in his head. He made a sudden decision.

Thomas Mannory was deeply contented. His two horses were his friends. He was known now in the town as a reliable, honest carter, and he had regular runs to and from the grain growing areas of Sussex. A day or two away fetching corn to the market and mills in Farnham pleased him, and he was always happy to be home at the Tanyard again, to give the horses free grazing in the water meadows, and to eat his mother's good meals.

For company he had young Hal as his assistant. Slight and wiry like himself, at sixteen Hal was a sturdy worker and brilliant with horses. Sometimes they walked beside the cart, sometimes one or both of them would ride. The cart, big with four wheels, and the pair which pulled it, were their pride and joy.

They had had a good run up from Chichester. Thomas was familiar with the best routes to take, avoiding steep hills both up and down, although long gentle rises could tax the horses and they would rest them at the summit before going on.

Today the sun was almost unclouded, yet not too hot. The road was in reasonable repair without mud patches or loose sand. Acquaintances had given cheery greetings as they passed, and some had offered welcome refreshment. Yet at times Hal seemed distracted. Thomas wondered if this was just his habitual silence, or something else.

They were on a level stretch so that both could ride the cart for a while. Thomas held the reins while Hal gazed at the distant horizon.

'There's a short job tomorrow,' Thomas said, 'Bricks from the kilns up Castle Hill, to go to where they're repairing the Castle.'

Hal nodded.

'You could take the small cart on your own, and the little horse.'

They reached the long rise from Horsham way, and dismounted to relieve the weight on the cart and urge the horses up it. At the hilltop they walked on for a while, and in the pleasure of a beautiful day and beautiful countryside, Thomas stopped thinking about bricks and carts and pondered his recent conversation with James. He knew more than James credited him with, sometimes flicking through the pamphlets he acquired. People should be free to believe and say what they thought right. Government should be more fair. And yet it seemed remote from ordinary daily life.

On another level stretch they were up on the cart again, and Hal pulled a crumpled piece of paper from his breeches pocket.

When nothing further happened, Thomas asked 'What do you have there?'

Hal said 'It's a letter from Abigail. I've had it a few days.'

'I didn't know my sister wrote to you,' Thomas said.

'She says I'm her adopted son.'

'Well,' Thomas said, 'I suppose you're sort of my brother anyway, since my father is said to have fathered you.'

Thomas flipped the reins to keep the horses going steadily. 'What does the letter say?'

Hal did not unfold it. He must have read it over and over again. He said, 'It just says they want to come back to Farnham.'

Thomas gave a sort of laugh. 'I thought Abigail must have gone for good. How long is it since she rode off on one of my horses?'

'Three years,' Hal said.

'Where was it again?'

'Why, Cropredy, where the battle was, and Ralph got wounded, and Mother Metcalfe took us in and healed him with her herbs and stuff and taught us harness-making, and then Abigail came and they married.'

It was an unusually long statement for Hal to make, and Thomas took a while to absorb the information, fitting it together with what he knew. Hal had been Ralph Attfield's 'paddy boy', with him through the war, taking care of his horse. And when word reached Abigail in Farnham that her sweetheart Ralph was wounded and lay way beyond Oxford, Thomas had lent her one of his horses so that she could go to him. Once she reached Cropredy, Hal left her with Ralph and rode the horse back to Thomas at the Tanyard, where he had remained.

Eventually Thomas said, 'So Ralph and Abigail have had enough of Cropredy and want to come back to Farnham.'

'Mother Metcalfe has died,' Hal said, 'and they have a babe, and could we go and fetch them?'

Thomas did not answer, for they had come to the ford at Shalford. He wanted to go slowly through it to allow the cart wheels to tighten their joints by soaking in the water. Hal pulled off his shoes and rolled up his breeches, glad to paddle and cool his feet as they crossed. Thomas stood watching, and thinking. To go so far would lose more days' work than he would like. That time when Abigail had borrowed his horse, she had told him that Cropredy was way beyond Oxford. It would be a good three days' journey, and another three days return, a whole week at least.

He crossed over the river on the flimsy foot bridge and called to the horses. They leant into their head collars and heaved the cart out of the water. Hal followed barefoot.

It was some days later that a letter came addressed to Thomas. Abigail had written it in haste and some excitement.

Dear Tom, she wrote. *We may have found an answer! Boats go down the Thames from Oxford, and the boatman says he could take us as far as Wallingford and could you meet us there? We can easily get from here to Oxford on a local cart. Dearest Tom, please do say yes, I long to see you all and be home.*

Wallingford. Thomas remembered the Thames-side town. It had been on the last leg of his longest journey, four years ago. He had left Farnham to carry a load to the troops in Bath, then went on with a load of royalist loot from Chippenham to Oxford, and then home again, passing through Wallingford on the way. Only a summer day's journey from Farnham to Wallingford if the horses were fit.

He tucked the letter into his breeches pocket and wandered into the meadow behind the Tanyard sheds. He needed to think, because recalling that journey nearly four years ago was surfacing other memories. The Army escort. The roadside farm. The terrified girl. He had wanted to go back. Now he wondered why, wondered what his going back could possibly accomplish.

His horses stopped their grazing and trotted up to him, expecting attention, expecting a titbit. He patted them absently, the memories becoming more and more vivid in his mind. Disappointed, the pair wheeled and trotted away, and for a moment he wanted to apologise to them. But they could not know how his thoughts were churning.

If he and Hal took them and the cart to Wallingford, Hal could drive it back again. Ralph was a horseman, they could do it together. And he himself could walk westwards until he found that farm by the roadside. He began to realise that now he would know no peace until he had found it, until he had returned as he had once hoped to do.

Chapter 2 - William Kiffin

'The Master's home!'

Hanna put her book down on the bed beside her in the Kiffins' London home, and made as if to rise.

'Nay, Mistress, he'll be up here in a moment. We've told him how it is.'

'Give me my comb then please. I am so disordered.' Hanna flicked the long golden plait forward over her shoulder, pulled at the strands, tried to comb where the pillow had tangled her fine hair – and he was there, bounding through the doorway as if he had not been all day in the saddle.

'Hanna! My darling!' His arms were around her, the sweet smell of him, the physical certainty of him. An end to anxiety.

He sat back on the bed, his big brown eyes holding her own as if gazing at each other would restore their intimacy, their unity.

Then, 'My sweet Hanna. I'm so sorry.'

Hanna grasped his hand. 'The birth was premature. Weeks before we expected. Yet she was alive. I had them make a little coffin. We blessed a corner of the garden and held a proper burial. Oh William, she was so tiny, so perfect, so real in the short time she lived.'

'I wish I had been here for you.'

'There's nothing you could have done.'

'Just to be here, and conduct the little funeral.'

Hanna shook her head. 'I've failed you so often. Shall I ever give you a son? Or even another daughter, one who survives?'

'Here's the one who has.' William looked towards the door where small fingers were curled around the frame, cautiously pushing it open. 'My little Lydia!' holding out his arms.

She was in his embrace in a moment, and he smoothing her silky hair, dark like his own.

'I thought you were asleep,' her mother said. 'It's quite late.'

'But it's so light. And I heard you talking.' The child disentangled herself. 'I even heard a bird singing.'

'May is a beautiful month, with blossom and new leaves, fresh.' William lifted his eight-year-old daughter onto his knee. 'I've been riding all around the West Country, and do you know what they grow there, little one?'

'Um, trees?' her mind still on the bird in the tree outside. 'No.'

'Flowers, like in Mama's garden?'

'No. They grow sheep. And what do sheep give us?'

Lydia clapped her hands. 'They give us wool!'

'And that's what I went there for; wool, fleeces, yarn, fabric, all products of our wonderful sheep.'

'But we don't have sheep, papa.'

'Thank God there are many who do, and they're glad to sell to me, to sell to merchants in Amsterdam, to earn the money that keeps you warm and fed.' He gave her a little squeeze.

'But why did you go away, for such a long time?'

'Well, it wasn't just wool.'

'What else then?' His daughter settled down as if for a story. William glanced at his wife who nodded encouragement. 'She is old enough to understand,' she said.

'At the end of January,' William said, 'we published our revised Confession of Faith, and the next month Thomas

Patience and I were summoned to appear before the Commission of Complaints in the House of Commons.'

'Complaints?' In all the unfamiliar words, this one alerted the child. 'What were they complaining about?'

'They are suspicious of us as Baptists.'

'They're not going to put you in prison, like in the White Lyon prison are they?'

'Why, you were barely three years old! Do you remember that?'

'Yes, but they won't, will they?'

'I hope not. Anyway, we decided that I should combine business with visiting the small congregations scattered about the country who hold that baptism is for believers, not for infants. So I took horse and went, as I said, around the West Country, which proved profitable in every way.'

'I'm not an infant.' Lydia wriggled herself free. 'When can I be baptised?'

William smiled at her. 'It's an important step to take. We'll talk about it later on.'

'And it's high time you were abed,' her mother said. 'Come,' to William, 'you must be hungry, and the servants will have prepared food for you. I'll just put on a wrap and come down with you.'

'Will you? I'd like that. Now little one,' William gave his daughter a hug which she knew had finality about it, 'off you go to bed and I'll see you in the morning.'

They sat down together to bread, cold capon and a jug of ale. William flicked through the pile of letters accumulated during his absence.

'Here's one from James Mannory,' breaking the seal on the

folded paper. 'Poor old James, always frustrated. Still at odds with his father. Thank God I'm my own master. Exceptionally good with the fine skins though.'

'He was full of ideals when he was apprentice in Southwark, wasn't he?'

'Southwark… I'm astonished that little Lydia remembers the White Lyon prison.'

'I think it's just that one time when I took her with me to visit you, and some of the prisoners burst into your cell, you remember?'

'I certainly do, armed with clubs and instructed to kill me.'

'And you welcomed them so sweetly that they changed their tune. But it affrighted Lydia, and the noise in the room below yours when the gang turned on the man who had set them to it. We have talked about it, but still sometimes she dreams about it and cries out.'

'Poor little one, pray God may take away this fear.'

Hanna broke off a knob of bread and nibbled it. 'Is it fear that makes people oppose the gospel truth?'

'Fear of allowing God to clean out our inner life?'

'Fear, which love can cast out…' Hanna said. 'Fear of little godly gatherings. Was it a fear that put you in prison?'

'Back then the Church hierarchy feared any rivalry to its control. Maybe losing control or power, is what is feared. Now Parliament is the body afraid of losing control. Look at the way writers and printers are hounded. The power of the printed word.' He poured more ale into his goblet. 'What news of our pamphlet writing friends?

'Still in prison. John Lilburne is in the Tower. Yet he manages to keep the printers busy with his scribblings. Richard

Overton too. He's still in Newgate gaol.'

'Both arrested without trial. We're no better off than when King Charles' Star Chamber operated.'

'And Will, their wives have been so kind to me. There's Elizabeth Lilburne lodging with John in the Tower with their children, scraping together something to live on. She relies on what is given to her, but I'm afraid some are falling away.'

'Some are impatient with John's broadsides. He can't resist inserting his own case. I wonder how Elizabeth endures his relentless pamphletting.'

'But she is constantly his messenger.'

'Willing to run risks. She's certainly a devoted help-mate.'

'More capon, Will? There is plenty.' He took a slice on the tip of his knife, as if he were still on the road.

'Mary Overton was in prison too. What of her?'

'She has been released, but of course she stays with Richard to look after him. Even she came to comfort me. Her babe died while it was with her in prison, yet she came to comfort me in my lesser loss.'

'I've read the petition Richard submitted on her behalf. "Poor little harmless innocent woman" he called her. But she must be made of sterner stuff than that.'

'She was only stitching some pamphlets Richard had printed when they arrested her. As she's with Richard in Newgate, their children remain with his sister. You remember their home was well nigh wrecked when the gang from the Stationers Company took her.'

'We must contribute to their needs.'

'I have given money to both her and Elizabeth.'

'Good lass. How can they live, lodged with wives and

children in prison and able to earn nothing?'

Hanna folded a cloth over the remnant of bread. 'I've tried to keep up with the newsbooks while you have been away. You'll hear best how things are from John and Richard themselves.'

William stood up, collected his papers and kissed her. 'I'll attend to these letters in the morning, and perhaps I'll write to James Mannory.'

William Kiffin was nine when his parents died. It was that hot hot summer of 1625, when the plague swept through London. His parents had repeatedly told him that God is good and loving, yet God had taken them, suddenly and horribly. Sick as they were they had sent him out of the city to relatives he scarcely knew, high up on Hampstead heath. When a breeze came it was cooler there, but still hot, and the heat wave lasted right through August, carrying off thousands of citizens both poor and rich.

There followed four unhappy years. The relatives tolerated him, using such resources as he had, (from which they also helped themselves) to support him and to school him. But he was haunted by his parents' death, haunted by himself being the one spared. Why had he not died along with them? Or supposing his father had risked losing business and taken them all three to Hampstead, might they be alive today? He speculated constantly on 'what if?' and whether God was there at all. The cautious look in his eyes, acquired during that time, remained into his adult life.

They apprenticed him to a glover. Making gloves was moderately interesting. At least it was a trade. At least he was back in London where he could consort with fellow apprentices.

He endured it for a couple of years until one day, bored and depressed with the prospect of a future as a glover but with no particular reason, he walked out.

It was very early on a Sunday. He had no idea where he was going. Wandering through familiar streets he turned into Budge Row. There a crowd of people was going into a church, St. Antholin's church. Beginning to be afraid at what he had done, and hungry for company, he entered with them.

The preaching stirred him. Here was a preacher steeped in knowledge of the Bible, a man who knew it, not just as theology, but who illuminated its relevance to life in the present. The theme that day was taken from one of the New Testament letters; 'The duty of servants to Masters'.

As the worship ended he stood, dazed, while the departing congregation flowed out around him, until three young men detached themselves, laughing, and stopped in front of him.

'Hullo!' said one. 'Come down from the clouds and introduce yourself!'

He looked at them, three men about his age, apprentices he may have seen as he went about the City, facing him and wanting to know him.

'Come!' said the jovial one, linking arms with him and spinning him round. 'Come and tell us why you look so solemn.'

They huddled together in the church porch, sheltering from the chill early morning wind, shuffling their feet when they got cold.

'*Why so pale and wan young lover, Prithee why so pale?*' the same lad asked.

'Hush, Richard,' one of them said, but he would not be hushed.

'Is it love or is it woe?' he asked.

'Neither,' William said. 'I feel… I've never heard scripture expounded so clearly. I feel…' He hesitated. These three might think him foolish if he told them what had happened.

'He's clear, isn't he, old Tom Foxley,' this from a tall lad with a thin face. 'Makes it make sense.'

Murmurs of agreement emboldened William. He would burst if he didn't tell somebody. 'I felt,' he said, 'as if he was talking just to me… as if, almost, that God was telling me what I need to do.'

'And what is that?' they asked. So he told them. Go back to my master. Which he did, as quickly and as quietly as he could, disturbing no one in the house.

But the encounter began their friendship. John Lilburne, the tall fine featured one, was apprenticed to a wholesale clothier, William Larner and Richard Overton to printers. Richard was the joker – 'You should see what he writes,' John said. 'Scurrilous sometimes and you can't help laughing.'

'There's good preachers in some churches,' Larner said. 'We go where they are.'

'And,' Richard added, 'We meet early every Sunday to delve into the Bible for ourselves.'

William joined them, warmed by their encouragement. They shared their doubts, their questions. They prayed. John seemed always tussling with inner problems. Richard made them laugh. Sundays filled with activity, for the afternoons were taken up with militia training out at Finsbury.

Their concern for spiritual truths fuelled their enthusiasm for social reform and justice. Time and again they joined the swarms of apprentices who poured down to Westminster or joined in protests in the City. Richard began to write and publish pamphlets, decrying the shortcomings of the church, the government, even sometimes the Independents, using his ready wit. John's earnest desire for justice, for himself and for the country, brought him into frequent trouble, in fact at one time it had bid fair to kill him.

'That James Mannory,' Will Larner said, 'the one we know at the artillery fields, the apprentice tanner. We should invite him along.'

Now William walked from his pleasant house in Moorgate, along the City wall down to Newgate Street and its dismal prison. He was ready with the coins the warder would expect in order to let him inside.

Richard Overton looked up from the small table where he was writing. 'Will! What a pleasure to see you!' He gathered papers off a stool. 'Pray sit down. I regret these two stools are all we have in our grand apartment.'

'At least you've not been clapped in irons again.'

'Ah! Those gangling spurs! The comeliest ever I wore in my life!'

'So you say, but you were glad to be freed from them.' William looked round the dark little room. 'Are you well treated here?'

'You see the delights of my lodgings, for which the gaoler has the kindness to take regular payments. Even those imprisoned for debt have to pay him. Truly a benevolent institution!'

'Come, have you enough to eat, and fuel?'

'My dear Mary is out foraging this instant.'

William perched on one of the stools. 'Last time I saw you

the matter was all *The Oppressed Man's Oppressions.'*

'Not my composition. John Lilburne's and he paid heavily for it. You know that the Stationers Company still claims a monopoly of printing. They sent their ruffians to raid his house, loaded three porters with his books and papers. We've all suffered from arrest and interrogations, whether at the House of Lords or the Commons. And yet neither has the right to make a man incriminate himself. Neither is a court of law. An Englishman's right is an open trial, answering declared accusations.'

'You've been acquainting yourself with the law of the land.'

'You know I've long been acquainted, though I've scant time for lawyers,' Richard said. 'Looking back though, one has to ask what progress has been made.'

'After all the fighting and loss, England seems to be no better,' William said.

'Take monopolies.' Richard got into his stride. 'They were meant to be abolished five years ago. How is it that the Stationers still have a monopoly of printing? Only they may print what is licensed, and licensed by whom? The King? Parliament? So they assume the right to raid our presses and imprison printers and booksellers.'

'Empowering their ruffians,' William said. 'I suppose we all guard power in our own way, and we fear when it is threatened.'

'So is that is why Parliament claims that our demands are libellous?'

Richard reached for a printed paper and waved it. 'You know of the petitions our friends in the City presented to the Commons while you were away?'

'Formulated by you?'

'I cannot claim that credit, though we did consult as far as we were able. This is now a third petition. The demands are not new. No more monopolies. No more arbitrary arrests. Debtors not to be imprisoned. You know the catalogue. Freedom of conscience, freedom of speech, freedom to print. The old law of England before the Conquest and the tyranny of Norman kings.'

'I don't know about Norman kings,' William said, smiling. 'That's a long time ago. Stuart kings are more our concern.'

'And now both Houses of Parliament are as protective of their power as ever was King Charles. So they ignored the first two petitions, and now this third one is prepared. John Lilburne persuades us that petitions are the way forward, and certainly many citizens do sign them.'

'Do you think this is the way we should be governed?'

'By petitions? Power resting on the people? Parliament to exist simply to enact their will expressed in petitions?' Richard scratched his head. 'I'm leaning towards that conclusion.'

'It could mean mob rule. That's the fear. Like fear of religious sects rising up, instead of the tight hold of the church, or control by a Presbyterian system of church rule.'

'That's on its way already,' Richard said. 'I wonder how readily it will be taken up.'

William sighed. 'Endless tensions and disagreements. Our faith should not be that way.' He turned as the door opened.

'Ah!' Richard said. 'Here is my Mary, laden with a feast!'

'Greetings Mistress!' William said. 'Neat and pretty as ever. However do you manage it?'

Mary bobbed a curtsey to William, kissed her husband and laid her small basket beside the fireplace.

'I met Thomas Lambe our pastor in Coleman Street – you're acquainted (turning to William) with his Independent congregation? He was telling me about this new petition, and they say we have the right to petition Parliament, and crowds go along to support them. But I expect you know all about that.'

'Thomas Lambe, how is he?' William asked.

'For all his politicking he is kind and generous as ever. He bought me some bread, and a little salt fish already cooked, and had my little basin filled with curds. He said that his congregation is mindful of us.'

'Your children,' William asked. 'Where are they?'

'They remain with Richard's brother. He and his wife are very kind, though even they have had to dodge the Stationers.'

'See how grateful for small mercies my Mary is!' Richard said.

'I've been away a month or more,' William said. 'It is time I made up for those weeks,' and he put a small bag of coins on the table. 'I'm glad to have talked with you Richard. I need to keep my eyes open in the City. Everywhere we turn there seems to be vying for power. God save us from such contention in our congregations, though Lord knows different sectaries clamour for attention.'

'Not just sectaries either! What about you and Lambe? He welcoming all into church membership, you limiting it to baptised believers?' Richard said.

'Oh you men!' Mary protested quietly. 'You take up positions and build a theology. Now come, Richard is hungry, and will you eat with us, William?'

'The Lord bless your food and your fellowship together. My Hanna will be expecting me home.'

Chapter 3 - Families

James' decision left him restless.

'I have one or two errands to do,' he told Jacob once he had seen everyone set to his tannery task, and he walked briskly to Castle Street, to the Garys' shop.

Christopher was fiddling around with bolts of cloth and looked up with some surprise at the unusual morning visit.

James blurted out, 'All well with your wife?' He had hoped to find Michael alone.

'As well as can be expected,' Christopher said. He waited to hear the real reason for James coming to the shop. They stood silently. Then James cleared his throat.

'I'd like a word with your father. Is he here?'

He was upstairs where he kept his stock, but came down quickly and gestured James into the back office. They stood there, surrounded by yet more cloth, Michael Gary expectant and impatient at this interruption so early in the day.

'Sir,' James said when the silent wait was becoming uncomfortable. 'Master Gary, I came to ask if I might court your daughter Ann.'

'Ann!' Gary said. 'What do you know of Ann?' He looked at James and then his eyes narrowed. 'Have you been meeting her secretly? I'll not stand for that!'

'No no, Sir,' James said hastily. 'No Sir, I know very little about her, but I have seen her in church, and I know the good reputation of your family.'

'You think you need a wife and you think my Ann would

be a good bet, eh?'

It was so accurate a surmise, even spoken in these aggressive tones, that for a moment James did not know how to answer.

Then he said, 'I would value your permission to make her acquaintance.'

Michael Gary nodded slowly. 'You had better come to the house this evening,' he said.

It wasn't just Ann, it was the whole family. James knew the house, where Snow Hill joined West Street, ideally placed for Betty Gary to know everything that was going on, and feeding her pride not to be living over the shop in Castle Street. He had never been inside. Hesitating outside the door he could hear a babble of voices, children's voices.

He knocked. It stopped.

The whole family it was indeed, Michael and Betty and their nine children. The panelled room could scarcely contain them, some crammed on the bench along one wall, hemmed in by the heavy oak table, the three girls across the end and the rest ranged along the free-standing bench. A pair of chairs with bright cushions was evidently reserved for the parents, but today one was occupied by Christopher's heavily pregnant wife. Thirteen people in all, with Betty perched on the end of the loose bench.

A small window let in the last of the evening light. One wax candle in its holder stood unlit in the centre of the table.

The smaller boys on either side of the girls jostled and shoved each other, while Eliza and Jane defended their patch at the end of the table with their fists. Ann sat between them, a hand on each shoulder, ineffectual restraint.

'Ow! You're squashing me!'

'Move round then.'

A biff from Eliza. 'He kicked me!'

'You hit me!'

Michael ignored the tumult, sat down in his chair and gestured James towards the end of the bench opposite his wife. But before he sat down James greeted Christopher and his wife Joan. They, whom he had known all his life, appeared as a quiet island in this sea of noise.

One of the smaller boys fished some coins out of his pocket and began to play Shove Ha'penny. Placing a ha'penny protruding just over the edge of the table he hit it with the heel of his hand so that it slid over the table top. His neighbour sent another after it, a good aim as it came to rest almost touching the first one.

'Give me one!' the smallest of the boys reached across the table. Ignoring him the first player sent a third coin sliding after the others. It went too far. His brother grabbed it.

'George!' bellowed Michael. 'Put those away!'

'Mike took my ha'penny!'

'Didn't.'

'You did. Give it me!'

Little Mike opened his hands. 'Haven't got it.'

'Where is it then?'

'On the floor.'

George and Nathanial slid off their bench and under the table. They groped in the near darkness around the tangle of feet and legs.

'Somebody's hiding it.'

'Hey, it's under your foot!'

'Take your foot off my ha'penny.'

'Ow! He's kicking me!'

Michael Gary stood up. 'Out!' he shouted. 'All of you, out! Nathanial, George, Mike, out!'

The miscreants emerged, clutching coins.

'And I'll have those coins.' Michael held out his hand.

Suddenly meek, they handed over their illicit wealth, then noisy again pushed each other out of the door.

Those who remained, collectively took breath. James sat down beside Christopher. Across the table Christopher's two next brothers were watching James intently. He met their gaze momentarily, aware of the three girls still sitting at the end of the table yet not somehow daring to look in their direction.

'So,' Michael said. 'A little peace.'

'Where did they get that money?' his wife said. 'Not that they're thieves, but they can't keep their fingers out of things, always up to something, I'm sure you older ones were never like that. Were you missing some money, husband?'

'Leave it,' Michael said. 'I'll deal with that later. James Mannory has come to meet the family.'

'Some introduction!' Christopher exclaimed. 'Joan is weary. Excuse us, please.'

James could hear their tread on the wooden stair going up to their bedroom. Everyone knew about the Great Bed Christopher had inherited and which filled that room. If I were married, James thought, I wouldn't care to live in a bedlam household such as this. Nor, for that matter, with his own family in Tanyard House with a loft full of apprentices and young journeymen. He would have to have a house, a place, of his own.

Out of the silence Michael cleared his throat. 'And how is business in the Tanyard?'

Betty, about to speak also, shut her mouth.

'Business?' James said. 'Oh, much as usual. The Army still needs shoes.' He would certainly not divulge his thoughts about the tanning business or his ambitions.

Another silence, but James had touched on young Robert Gary's passion.

'Father said you were in the Army,' he blurted out.

'Just the London Auxiliaries,' James said.

'What's the London Auxiliaries then?'

'Part time soldiers, apprentices and such. We trained weekly.'

'What, with muskets and cannons?'

'With muskets. Ordnance was my responsibility.'

'Gunpowder?' Robert sounded awed.

'Gunpowder, among other things,' James said.

'Robert has a passion for anything military,' Betty broke in. 'He has quite a collection of bits and pieces picked up in the Park, and what he doesn't know! It's remarkable.'

'Auxiliaries. Not the New Model Army,' Robert persisted.

'It was before that was set up.'

'But you were in some battles?'

Reluctantly, James said, 'Yes.' Then he smiled at Robert. 'It was a long time ago. Four years at least.' He turned towards Michael. This was scarcely a way to approach Ann.

'Eliza,' Betty said, 'Fetch the tinder box.' She turned to James. 'We find we need wax candles in this room with the dark panelling. And with rush lights the smell of tallow taints the cushions and such.'

46

A sign of some wealth, James thought, and found himself speculating on what dowry Ann might bring to her marriage.

Eliza handed the tinder box to Ann. Carefully and skilfully she made a flame and held it to the candle wick. The momentary flare of light lit up her face, held still, intent on her task. A chance to watch her unobserved. She set the candle back in its holder.

The solitary candle's light gave a new warmth to the room. The flame flickered, reflected in the polish of the table. It made everything beyond its circle shadowed, dim. Conversation was desultory as eyes were drawn to the candle. Michael received Betty's recurrent titbits of news and opinion more kindly. And still Ann had not spoken a word.

In the veiled light James felt emboldened to look at her again. He wondered if the calm look on her face was truly calm, or was it blank. What was she thinking? Her little sisters were quiet, the younger one nearly asleep, her head lolled against Ann's breast. Ann had her arm around her.

Seeing that, he suddenly found himself imagining her arm around himself, but without that neat dress, imagining her warm smell, imagining his head resting on her bare breast. Almost ashamed to be so aroused and in company, he yet kept gazing at her.

The picture he was savouring, of her naked embrace, must have shown in his eyes, for momentarily she looked up and held his gaze. Her expression sent a thrill right through him.

No words were needed, after all.

Nonetheless, the following Sunday James winkled her out of her family, with her father's connivance, to walk her home from church the longer route. In fact it was not the way to her home at all, but a wander across the meadows, over the bridge at Weydown mill, and back along Weydown Lane towards the Tanyard itself. Much of the time they walked in silence.

As they left the church yard however, James said, 'I'd like to live in one of those houses in Church Lane.' Ann made no comment so he thought he should elaborate. 'Away from the tannery and handy for the town. Not far from the currier too.'

'The baker is along there,' Ann said, and looked surprised when he said, 'My mother makes all the bread we eat.'

They walked on along the meadow paths towards the mill. Somewhat abruptly he said, 'Can you cook?'

'Mother is famous for her plum cake,' Ann said.

'And you?'

She looked as if no one had ever asked her that before. After a while she said, 'I suppose so. It can't be very difficult.'

'Who cooks at home?' James asked.

'The maid does mostly, and my mother. She likes me to mind the children.'

James began a mental inventory. Someone would need to teach her the rudiments of cooking; his mother Phoebe perhaps who produced meals with little apparent thought. On the other hand Ann would know how to care for babes when they came along. He did not want to dwell on that, he wanted her body exclusively for himself, and he would not care to see it in a distended condition like Joan's. With every step they took across the meadows, feeling her beside him, being able to look at her as she walked, his desire for her became more urgent.

They stopped by the gate into the Tanyard, the two mastiffs chained there barking first a warning and then a welcome.

James hushed them.

'I'm Foreman here, as you probably know,' he said. 'The hides are brought into the yard and taken down to the river to be washed, and then they go into the lime pit before having all the fat and flesh scraped off them. Then they go into the first of the tanning pits, you can see those, with the poles across the pits, and the hides are suspended from the poles. They have to be moved regularly, each pit has a greater concentration of tannin in it. The oak bark is shredded in that shed over there, and...

He glanced at Ann. She had a kerchief over her nose.

He laughed. 'You get used to the smell,' he said. 'It's strongest when new hides are brought in from the shambles.' He gestured across the yard to the sheds along one side. 'When the tanning is complete the hides have to be scoured and smoothed and cut to shape. Over a year it takes if the leather is to be durable and waterproof.'

'I'd like to go home.' Ann's voice was muffled by the kerchief.

James stopped in full flow. This was his trade, his livelihood. The processes were of great interest. At least, to him. For a moment he looked at her, uncomprehending. Then he touched her elbow and moved them both away towards the bridge.

'We wouldn't have to live there,' he muttered.

'We?' Ann stopped, mid-bridge.

He stopped too, and faced her. If only that look he had caught in candlelight would come back into her eyes.

'I've asked your father if I may court you. I want you for my wife.'

She looked him up and down, an appraising look. Then

she laughed, the first time he had heard her laugh, a laugh he could not interpret.

'You're very quick,' she said.

Hal led the horses into the tannery yard, setting the cart on the level space between the lane gate and the tanning pits.

Ralph Attfield climbed carefully out of the cart. Abigail handed down their little sleeping son and almost before her feet touched the ground she was wrapped in her mother's embrace.

'Let me look at you!' Phoebe held her away, hands on her shoulders. 'Three years and you're just the same!'

Abigail grinned. 'A little more matronly?'

'Nay, you'll never grow to my girth. And the little lad, let me hold him.' But the child had begun to waken and wanted his mother.

'This is Simon,' Abigail said, presenting him to the household members who had been hanging around in the tannery yard through the long May evening, awaiting their arrival. The child surveyed them, then rubbed his eyes and nuzzled his head into her neck.

'Father?' Jacob seemed to be holding back. He came forward then, held her hand in both of his and kissed her lightly on her forehead.

He turned to Ralph saying 'Welcome!' At that the resident tanners, journeymen and apprentices, who had stood back in a shy circle, were emboldened to peer openly at Ralph. They had heard tell of the wounds he had sustained at the Battle of Cropredy Bridge, and now they saw the scars for themselves. From the right side he looked much as he always had done, jaw firm, full lips over fine teeth, but the left side of his face carried a deep scar from ear to chin. Some teeth were missing and the skin was pulled askew. The onlookers scarcely noticed that he also limped.

When Ralph and Abigail had met with Thomas and Hal at Wallingford, the first exclamation had been how tall Hal had grown in the three years since he had exchanged his place at Cropredy with Abigail. He was no longer the skinny orphan who had tended Ralph's horse and become like a son to him. As they drove the next day, they had talked themselves back into an easy relationship.

Now they moved indoors, Jacob and Phoebe with servants and workers all joining in this momentous return. Phoebe picked a rush light out of the box beside the hearth, lit it from the tinderbox and clamped it in its stand. Abigail loosened her bodice and suckled little Simon.

'Where is James?' she asked.

'Oh... Phoebe hesitated. James must be left to tell his own news, whatever he had. 'He'll be back before dark. But isn't Thomas with you?'

'He left us at Wallingford,' Ralph said. 'Some errand he'd set his heart on.' They settled to bread and cheese and ale.

'I know it's late,' Ralph said as he ate, 'but I'd like to tell you our plans.'

'Ah! Here's James!' Phoebe interrupted. 'Now he can hear them too.'

'We've exchanged letters with various people here,' Ralph said. 'We've arranged to rent a small house in West Street, or even buy it if it proves suitable.'

'It has a work room, and two bedrooms upstairs, so Hal will be able to live with us,' Abigail said.

'What work do you plan to do there?' Jacob asked.

'Oh, harness making. We've been making a living at that these several years, under Mother Metcalfe's watchful eye. She taught us. When she died we found she'd left us all her tools.'

James looked from one to the other, definite in what they intended to do, free to do it even if they had to clear some formalities with the Burgesses. Leatherwork too. If only he could be free to develop the curing of fine skins.

Ralph sought out Jacob one afternoon when the tannery seemed to be looking after itself. Three years living in Mother Metcalfe's simple dwelling had left him unused to stairs and he reached the office out of breath.

'Come in, come in!' Jacob said, offering him a stool.

'Thank you. I'll need to strengthen my legs if I'm to keep up with young Simon as he grows.' He looked round, noting the ledgers, quills and ink and the neatness of the small room. 'I'm proud, Sir,' he said, 'to be able to call you father-in-law.'

'About Hal,' he said. 'Abigail and I would like to treat him as our son. Adopt him, I suppose. For that I think we'd need your consent.'

Jacob took time to absorb this. Then he said 'Because I'm supposedly his father?'

'Well, yes. But also because, isn't he your employee?'

'Oh no. I relinquished him to you when you took him as your paddy boy. Since he's been back here he's worked with Thomas. Thomas pays him a wage, I believe.'

'He's sixteen. I'd like to have him apprenticed, to a saddler or a horse collar maker, so that he can work alongside me in our harness-making business. He's already competent with

52

harness-making. I'd like to have these trades under one roof.'

'You sound like James, all for expansion and change.'

'Nay, I'll move slowly. We have to gain people's confidence with good work. And it'll be seven years before Hal would be qualified.'

'Those who know you, know you as a horse dealer.'

'Maybe I'll do that a little, one day. But not riding with a string of horses from fair to fair. This leg is troublesome.'

'So you're asking me if you may take a father's responsibility for young Hal.'

'We'd like him to live with us, if you agree.'

'My dear son-in-law, in truth it has nothing to do with me. Hal lived here as a child, then he followed the Army with you. Naturally when he left you at Cropredy he lodged here. But it is Thomas who employs him. You'll have to talk to Thomas.'

'We last saw Thomas at Wallingford over a week ago. What has become of him?'

Hal wanted to know that too. Thomas kept a rough record of orders in the stable. Hal hesitated for several days before he looked in it, and what he saw worried him. He ventured to take it to Ralph.

'Look, it's one of the gunpowder orders for the garrison here at the Castle. We don't get those so often now the fighting's finished.'

'Will you do that run on your own?'

'I'd prefer not to with the big cart. And we'd need the big cart and both horses.'

'No one you know who could help?'

'No one I like.'

'Like?'

'Well, trust. I couldn't ask you, could I?'

'I'm not a carter.'

'We worked well on the way from Wallingford.'

'Hal, I want you to learn a trade so that we can work properly together. Saddler or collar maker, that's what I want for you. Not to spend your days as assistant carter.'

Hal stood still, digesting this, clutching the order book.

'But for now,' he said at last, 'that's what I am. And Thomas isn't here. And I don't know what to do.'

Betty Gary's nose for gossip had its uses.

'I hear,' James said, returning from one of his frequent visits to the Gary home, 'I hear that Abe Trussler hasn't paid his fine.'

Jacob grunted. 'The Burgesses are not pressing him for the time being,' he said.

'I must say, he seems in a sorry state,' James said. 'I saw his yard a while back, not much going on, and his cart wheel damaged.'

Hal neither liked nor trusted Abe Trussler. Violent and wily, Abe had always, in their encounters, been against him. But he was at least a carter of sorts.

Swallowing his fear, Hal took himself along to Abe's yard, puzzling as he went how best to approach him.

Abe had propped up his cart in order to remove the offending wheel, so far without success. Hal stood watching, familiar with the ways of carts. He went forward and said quietly, 'Can I help… Sir?'

Abe grunted without looking up, and together they heaved the wheel off its axle, an easier task for two. Abe propped the wheel against the side of the cart and only then 'Oh! It's you,' he said. 'What are you doing here, bastard Mannory?'

All those years of antagonism just because of who he was.

'I came,' Hal said hesitantly, 'to ask your help.'

'Hah!' Abe snorted. 'That's a new one!'

'Thomas… Thomas is away. He's been delayed. There's an order to collect gunpowder from Chilworth. I'm wary of doing it on my own.'

'So?'

'I wondered if you would help me.' Hal looked round the decrepit yard, remembered the unpaid fine and added, 'I'll be paid so we'd share the pay.' Surely Thomas wouldn't mind.

He could sense conflicting emotions at work in Abe. They stood eyeing each other, saying nothing. Hal had never before taken an initiative such as this. He was in unknown territory and desperately wanted it to succeed.

At last Abe blurted out 'Tomorrow?'

Chapter 4 - To the Farm and a Riot

Thomas had been walking for two hot days, his carter's smock stuffed into a bag on his shoulder which had little else still in it. He had installed Ralph and Abigail with their babe and Hal in the Wallingford Inn for the night, and then, impatient to be off, had set out in the fading light of the long May evening.

Guided by advice from chance encounters on the way, he guessed that he had not always been given the most direct route, but now he was on the Oxford road, casting about for whether to go right or left, towards Oxford or westwards.

It was a cross-roads which decided him, a cross-roads with a sign post to Chippenham. That must be the way to the roadside farm, to his destination. Encouraged, he set off again.

But his confidence was waning with every step he took. What could he say? Why had he come? What excuse could he make for intruding on their life? He could find no rational reason for the compulsion that had been driving him here.

Then suddenly he realised he had arrived. He recognised the house, the yard, the barn, the cowshed, less changed than he had dared to hope.

And he was very thirsty.

The old woman who answered his tentative knock had not changed either. Stout and formidable, she looked him up and down.

'Water it is, is it?'

'If you please, ma'am. I've walked a long way, and it's hot.'

'A tramp, eh. Selling some cheap trash I dare say.'

'No, ma'am, I've nothing to sell.'

'Then what's in that sack?'

'Just some clothes.' Thomas reached into the bag and pulled out his leather water bottle, long since dry. 'I'd be very grateful for some water to drink.'

He held the bottle out to her. Seeing its quality she softened slightly, though he could tell she half suspected he had stolen it.

'Wait here,' she said.

She watched him slowly drink it. Her gaze made him aware of his dusty boots and breeches, of two days' growth of beard, of his untidy hair under his cap. He stoppered the bottle and replaced it in the bag.

He couldn't just go on standing there, and the woman, hands on hips, was making no move. The best idea seemed to be to ask, 'Is there any work I could do?'

'Is there any work you <u>can</u> do?' she replied. 'You vagrants…'

Thomas swallowed hard. Did he look like one of the relicts of the armies, deserters, or discharged with no trade but that of killing?

'Any… labouring work?' he ventured, standing straight.

She seemed to be considering. Then she said, 'They're hoeing and weeding up yonder. Mayhap they can use you.'

There were fields of peas, and of beans, and fields of what he supposed were turnips, and people dotted about in them.

A swarthy man not much older than himself spotted him. 'You wanting work? We're short today. Can you use a hoe?'

'I've never done so.'

He shrugged. 'Go along a fresh line of bean plants beyond

the others,' he said, 'and pull the weeds. Mind you don't pull up beans as well.'

Pulling the weeds used an unaccustomed set of muscles, but however tired he might be, here was a chance to be alongside the farm workers, the family members. They worked hard, well into the evening. Then the man who had told him what to do, called a halt and everyone started back towards the farmyard.

He came up to Thomas. 'I don't know who you are, but you've made yourself useful. You'd best come and eat with the rest.'

They crowded into the farm kitchen where a woman and a girl helped the old one serve ale and simple food. The woman, he guessed, was her daughter, and the younger one, aged perhaps about fifteen, a grand-daughter. Of the old man with the long white beard whom Thomas remembered, there was no sign.

No one dismissed him nor did anyone ask him where he would sleep, though he sensed an assumption that he would work again the next day. No matter, the night was warm and he had already slept under the stars on his way here. He settled himself under a tree, and slept profoundly.

It was the pea field next day, bending and pulling as before, and stacking the weeds. Sometimes a cart was brought along and they piled them in, a change of action which gave relief to Thomas's weary back. At midday the old woman came with a servant bringing bread, cheese and ale, and the workers gathered in the shade to refresh themselves.

'Not seen you before,' the man sitting on the ground next to Thomas said. 'What brings you here?'

'I…' Thomas hesitated. 'I called in here once, some years ago.'

'You travel this road much then?'

'No, it was only that once.' Thomas took a deep breath. 'During the fighting hereabouts.'

'In the Army were you?'

Drat the persistence of the man. And they had been overheard. The swarthy man who had given him work looked with narrowed eyes from where he was sitting close by, and said, 'In that troop that caused such havoc in this place?'

Before Thomas could bring himself to answer, his former questioner wanted the full story – the troop, the havoc, what had happened that seemed so memorable. But the other shook his head.

'I wasn't there in fact,' he said. 'Margie ran out to us in the field – it must have been haymaking time. She warned us not to come back, though I'd have been glad to deal a few blows at those troopers, the blackguards.'

Margie spoke up. 'Yes, I saw them arrive and went to warn the men. If you were one of those troopers you'll not be welcome here, however hard you work.'

Thomas could feel animosity building up around him. That night was still vivid in their memories. It might have happened yesterday, so strong was their indignation. The anger and bitterness was palpable.

Thomas felt unable to defend himself. He sat still, saying nothing, looking down.

Then he heard a little gasp, and a girl's voice said, 'I know who he is!'

All attention was suddenly on her. He looked up and saw the young lass, blushing now, silenced by the attention.

'Who is he then?' Margie asked. 'Tell us, Charity.'

'He's…' Charity spoke so quietly they could hardly hear her. 'He's… the carter… the wrestler.'

The matriarch cornered him as the workers returned to the fields. 'Wrestler eh?' she looked him up and down. 'Wrestler!' she repeated scornfully. 'You hardly look the build for a wrestler. Where did she get that idea?'

Thomas stood his ground, silently.

'Never know what she's thinking.' She shook her head. 'I had to raise her. That reckless man who fathered her went off to some outlandish place and left the child with us. I feared she'd become just like her mother (God rest her soul). Her mother died, you see. Charity used to be inquisitive, into everything. But since your Army troop invaded my farm, she hardly speaks.'

'I wasn't in the Army,' Thomas felt constrained to say. 'I'm a carter, and they'd contracted with me to take a load of loot to Oxford. The troopers were an escort, to protect it.'

'Protect!' a mocking half laugh. 'They drank every drop of ale in the house, stole all my cheeses, killed my goose, commandeered every bed. My husband and I passed the night in the woodshed. Lord knows what they got up to with Charity – stubborn wench, she stayed in the house.'

Thomas nodded.

'So what brought you back here, digging up all that misery?'

Thomas swallowed. Why had he come? Hesitantly, he said, 'For a long time I've felt I needed to come back. I don't know why.'

'Is it Charity you want?'

'I just wanted to find some sort of conclusion.'

'You wanted to see Charity?'

How could he answer that? He had not even recognised her from such a fleeting memory. When he did not reply, the old woman started walking down to the farmhouse, talking as she went.

'You could be anyone,' she said. 'Carter without a cart.'

'I'm Thomas Mannory. I drove my cart to Wallingford, to allow my sister to move her family and goods to Farnham where I live. Being part way here, I walked on.'

'Leaving your sister to drive the cart?' she mocked.

'Her husband and my assistant,' Thomas said.

The catechism continued over the next few days, questions about his circumstances, his standing, his family. Then about the third morning, speaking as someone who expected to be obeyed, she said, 'I have decided to send Charity to Farnham with you. Your mother can put her to work, in this tannery house you speak of. It is time she left the farm.'

The Kiffin household was astir early as usual the twentieth morning of May. Not a bright morning, but cloudy with a threat of rain as so many days had been lately.

William put an arm round Hanna's shoulders as she sat braiding Lydia's long dark hair, and kissed the top of her head. 'I am going to the Warehouse,' he said.

'Be watchful,' Hanna said. 'Every day people pour down to Westminster, and I am wary of crowds.'

'Apprentices again? When I was apprenticed we crowded to anything that was afoot, especially unjust arrests.'

'Not only apprentices, I believe.'

'How do they ever get any work done!'

Hanna shrugged. 'Passions are high. And so are prices.'

'I realised that as I travelled. Poor harvests, and many hungry.'

Lydia looked round. 'Why are they hungry? Why don't they just buy food?'

'Poor harvests mean a shortage of food.'

'But we always have food.'

Faced with poverty, William often felt uncomfortable with his own surprising prosperity, but he said 'We have been blessed with wealth, but poor people cannot afford to buy when prices are high.'

'Is that why they are rioting?'

William squatted down to her level. How to begin to explain to his daughter the struggles which the late wars had done nothing to resolve? 'Shall we say they are passionate for justice?'

'Their demands seem reasonable enough to me,' Hanna said, almost ignoring her daughter's curiosity. 'And they have their heroes, printers and publishers like Overton, Tew and Browne.'

'They're certainly heroic,' William said.

He kissed wife and daughter again, pulled on a workaday leather jerkin, and set out.

The streets did seem more populated than usual. He cut through the smaller streets towards St Paul's. There groups were coalescing before moving off westward, others simply tagging along. He spotted an acquaintance.

'Good day, Tim,' he said. 'What is the issue today?'

'Will Browne. He's to be questioned today by the House of Commons.'

'So he was finally arrested, then?'

Tim laughed. 'The Stationers' Company gang came once too often. He'd twice given them the slip.'

William fell into step beside him. The warehouse could wait a day. Tim went on, 'Parliament only bothers about who are the writers and the printers of what keeps us informed. And has them arrested.'

'Remarkable how swiftly letters and pamphlets are printed and distributed,' William said.

'You'd think those members of Parliament can't read. Petition after petition they've been given and they ignore them.'

'Two months they've had that last petition,' someone nearby said, 'and have they read it?' Men nearby brayed their agreement.

They had reached the top of Ludgate Hill. The ever increasing crowd flowed around them along Fleet Street, some in an almost festive mood, others already angry, but united by a sense of right on their side.

William knew Will Browne, not intimately but with liking and respect. A brave publisher and book seller, he was clearly the hero of the moment.

Low tide had left stretches of mud below the Strand, mud dotted with boats at odd angles. The narrowed Thames hovered, apparently movelessly, between tides. Then where the river course curved away they entered Whitehall, and some young men started running, urging each other on, towards the old Palace of Westminster.

Only parts of the Palace had remained after the destructive fire many years ago. The House of Lords met in one room, and there were adjacent committee rooms. The Commons met in the old St Stephen's church. The crowd outside its doors was thickening fast. They jostled for space. Those in front shouted out for justice, for freedom. Others shouted for their petitions.

One or two of the boldest ventured inside the doors. William hesitated, but then he slipped inside after them.

A high solid wooden screen separated the entrance lobby from the main body of the church, the Chamber, a screen with a door on either side. Only the louder voices penetrated the screen, yet clearly an interrogation was going on. To force a prisoner to incriminate himself – they did that all the time, the Lords, the Committee of Examinations, the Commons, and it was against the law.

William could hear ever louder questions being flung at Browne who evidently was refusing to reply.

One of the men who had come in with William went outside and shouted to the crowd, about what was going on. A cry of 'Petition! Petition!' started and rapidly spread. Suddenly those in the front of the crowd pushed him aside and burst through the doors into the lobby. William flattened himself against a wall as men surged round him. Now the cry was 'Justice! Freedom!' with growing anger.

Someone from inside the Chamber opened one of the screen doors a crack. An expectant hush within before he nipped back. In the lobby ears strained to make out words in the babble of voices. They heard a loud voice making a proposal. There were cries of 'Yea!' and a pause. Then the screen doors opened and Members streamed through the Yea door, propelling the crowd before them and shouting 'Clear the lobby!'

Rioters and Members converged in a melee outside.

Members attempted to slip away unnoticed. A spokesman came and stood still on the entrance steps. He raised his hand and waited while the hubbub subsided.

Then over their heads he shouted, 'This new petition is deemed to be seditious, scandalous and a high breach of privilege. Along with the earlier petitions, it is to be burnt by the public hangman.'

There was a stunned silence. A moment of balance – would they become a mob and storm the Chamber, or would the habit of authority restrain them? A rumble of dissent spread through the crowd. Leveller leaders had worked hard on that petition, invested with a passion for justice. Others in the crowd had gone along to support Will Browne. But the door was bolted shut, and eagerness drained out of them. They began to disperse.

'I need to visit John Lilburne,' William said, and walked down through the City towards the Tower, away from the crowd. He was not ready to tell Hanna where he had been, what he had witnessed, until he knew more.

Gaining entry to the Tower of London was easy, without too much greasing of palms. He had visited John Lilburne during other of his spells in prison, for no sooner was John let out on bail than he raised fresh fury against himself. Younger than Richard Overton but contemporary with William, clean shaven with a neat moustache, he was beloved by women despite a damaged eye, and a popular hero. Everything that came from his prolific pen he contrived to get printed on the secret presses, and rapidly distributed. Here in the Tower he was like a caged tiger.

'So,' William said, knowing John's impatience with small talk, 'The petitions are to be burnt. All your work going up in smoke.' He sat down on a stool.

John looked at him keenly. 'Where have you been these last months? We've only seen Hanna, bless her, when she comes to bring provisions to Elizabeth.'

'And Hanna blesses Elizabeth, for her dear visit after the baby died.'

'And where were you?'

'In the West Country, on business here and there. And visiting Baptists to encourage them. Now be pleased to tell me all that has been happening,'

'Where to begin? You'll have read *The Outcries of the Oppressed Commons* which was published the last day of February? It was my response to the House of Commons' refusal to receive a petition. I included a request for our release from prison, myself and Richard Overton among others. A thousand signatures that petition had.'

'I read that pamphlet of yours just after Thomas Patient and I were up before the Committee of Complaints.'

'Parliament shows no interest in what is being asked for. All they want is to know who wrote and published it, to clap them in prison.'

'Then there was the large petition, wasn't there?'

'The London Levellers compiled that. They've banded together with a regular subscription and a Treasurer. Pity they've acquired that name. We're not asking to level everyone down. All we ask is for justice, fairness.'

'You had a hand in that petition, surely,' William said.

'Oh yes, along with Nicholas Tew, and good old William

Walwyn in the background as usual. He's a wise old bird and he shares our aspirations, but he prefers to keep out of view.'

'So what were the demands?'

'You know our principle concerns. I have a rough copy of the petition here. First of all it says how we had hoped that we should soon be delivered from all oppression over soul and body. That was our hope, after expending so much time, blood and treasure, and many families having experienced ruin, yet, I quote, 'we still find the Nation oppressed with grievances of the same destructive nature as formerly, though under other notions.'

'That's a direct attack on this Parliament, which seems to be sitting for ever,' William said.

'Well, it's true. The way power is exercised has not changed since the days of King Charles and the Star Chamber. Only now it's in the hands of the Lords, and the Presbyterians in Parliament.'

'There must be positive demands as well as this complaint.'

'Most certainly. You will readily agree that we must have religious freedom. All laws must be in English, not in archaic Latin. No one should be forced to incriminate himself in whatever court. All monopolies without exception must be abolished – yes, you'll identify with that. And criminals should receive humane treatment, with no imprisonment for debt.'

'All most reasonable,' William said. 'I surmise it was the attack on the present Parliament which was resented.'

'Resented!' John exclaimed. 'The House of Commons treated the petition as a libel, and when Tew spoke up he was arrested. So then a second petition was prepared, desiring the whole affair to be looked into, with Tew released and the right of petitioning to be recognised. How else can the people reach the ears of members of Parliament who are meant to be representing us?'

'That must have been toward the end of March.'

'Exactly so. The London group prepared yet another petition which asked for Tew's release and questioned the right of a Committee of the House of Commons to commit anyone to prison. Then Browne spoke out his impatience and was arrested. The rest you know. Crowds at Westminster the day Tew was to be questioned. The House of Commons, not bothering to read the petitions, and…'

'I've just come from there,' William broke in. 'They've declared that petition seditious, scandalous and a high breach of privilege. The petitions are to be burnt by the common hangman.'

'I ask you!' Lilburne exclaimed. 'A panic decision. All they bother about is their own position, their status. They're meant to represent the people but will they listen to the people? The common hangman to burn them you say! How self serving is that! Doubtless there'll be crowds to watch that spectacle as well, but what good do they do?'

William moved to look out of the small window, though not so much looking outwards as ruminating internally. 'Did you ever read Bishop Lancelot Andrews' sermons?' he said. 'He lived, what, a hundred years ago. I was struck by part of one sermon which I committed to memory and I have often returned to it. He said "A false conceit is crept into the minds of men, that the points of religion that be manifest are certain petty points. These, yea these, be great and none but these, that have great disputes about them. It is not so. Those that are necessary God hath made plain; those that are not plain, not necessary".'

'Do you live by that?' John countered. 'You have held frequent debates with those who disagree with your tenets about baptism.'

'I don't deny it. I was simply thinking that we all, even Bishop Laud with all his ceremonial, and Presbyterians and Independents, believe the basic facts of our faith. Differences become political when it comes to how the church is organised, where the power lies. What difference is there between the rule by bishops, and the Presbyterian model of a national church?'

'Little if any.'

Lilburne turned back to his own urgent concerns. 'I've encouraged petitioning, but I confess I'm losing heart. I'm going to the people and to the Army.' He reached for one of the latest newsbooks. 'Only days ago my faithful contacts in the Army brought copies of a letter from eight regiments of horse, eight cavalry regiments no less, which was read in the House. And then within days the Commons handed over control of the City Militia to the City of London, Presbyterians too.' John Lilburne started striding around his little room. 'Eighteen thousand men at City and Parliament's disposal!'

'And the Army, the New Model Army…?'

'Parliament wants to disband most of it and send the rest to Ireland, with a pitiful amount of the pay owed.' Ignoring the newsbook, John picked up his latest diatribe, *Plain Truth without Fear or Flattery.* 'As I said, I'm appealing now to the whole nation and to the Army. There's cohesion in the Army and a sense of purpose.'

Wearied by Lilburne's vehemence, William turned to a related topic. 'You used to have frequent meetings with Oliver Cromwell.'

'Cromwell! He's politician as well as General, that's the trouble. He's one of the Commons committee that keeps flitting back and forth to Saffron Walden to negotiate with the Army. Seems to want to please everyone. We used to meet regularly, he coming to the Tower, but I've fallen out with him lately.'

William smiled quietly at John's recurring ability to fall out with people. But all he said was 'As General or as Politician?'

'Both I suppose. Worshipping as an Independent, he's at odds with all those Presbyterians in the Commons, and Lord knows what he is trying to achieve with the Army. Our Agents go back and forth and tell of his visits to one regiment after another. The Agents do keep the Army and the City Levellers in close touch.'

'You've quite an organisation going by the sound of it,' William said. 'No wonder Parliament is uncomfortable.'

'So they should be!' John Lilburne exclaimed.

Chapter 5 - Charity and a wheel

'I've brought you an orphan,' Thomas said. That was all. He held the reins of the hired horse, adjusted his hold. A woman stood in the doorway of the little house, a child on her hip, her brown hair untidy under her cap, her apron marked. Charity clasped her bundle, daring only a glance.

Then the woman said 'Oh Tom!' like a gentle reproof. A moment later her tone changed. 'We've only the furniture from Cropredy. You'll need to fetch a bed of some sort from the Tanyard, if Mother can spare one.'

'I'll see to that,' Thomas said, and led the horse away, all settled so quickly as if handing a person over to a total stranger were an ordinary everyday occurrence. Charity gazed after Thomas, her tenuous anchor in this bewildering day, seemingly casting her adrift.

Grandmother had said, 'You're to go to Farnham with Thomas Mannory here.'

'With… Thomas?' she had stammered.

'Margie and Ned will go with you. Ned knows the way, and where to change horses.'

'My mother will find somewhere for you to stay,' Thomas had assured her.

But enduring that uncomfortable journey, two days perched pillion behind Thomas on a series of horses, catching snatches of conversation, Charity's apprehension had grown. Wasn't Thomas' home a tannery full of men? And his mother could not have been warned that he was bringing her.

Suppose she said 'No!' Suppose she knew nowhere Charity could lodge, even for a night. Thomas was her only hope – and he had gone!

A woman had been drawing water from a conduit at the foot of a broad street below a Castle. Thomas enquired of her.

'The Mannory girl come back with the horse dealer?' she had said. 'Just moved in. Next to the White Hart Inn.'

Thomas had told Ned and Margie to wait, and brought her here – and left.

'I'm Abigail.' The woman drew her into the house. 'My brother didn't give you much of an introduction. What is your name?'

'Charity.' Little more than a whisper, her eyes on the littered floor.

'It's a mess at present,' Abigail said, following her gaze. 'There is a lot we haven't stowed yet. We only moved in here a couple of days ago.' She gestured to some of the sacks which smelt faintly of leather. 'We're harness makers. This room will be our workshop.' She put the child down. 'Come Simon, let's show Charity where we live.'

A stairway led steeply up between the front and back rooms, the back room no larger than the other but more organised with some pans on a shelf and a clean fireplace. Abigail gestured Charity to a stool and sat down herself.

'I grew up in Farnham,' she said, 'but I've been away these three years, north of Oxford where there was a battle. My husband was a soldier. He'll be home soon.'

She turned her attention to little Simon, playing a hand game with him.

A soldier! Charity cringed. She sat, still clutching her cloth bundle.

And then the street door opened and there was Thomas with a tall young version of himself, carrying a set of longer and shorter struts between them.

'We've brought one of the beds from the loft,' Thomas said. 'It's quick to re-assemble. Where shall we take it?'

'The room at the back,' Abigail said, 'it's empty. We'll stay down here, there isn't space up there for more than a couple of people.'

'Up we go then Hal,' Thomas said, and they manoeuvred the wooden struts up the narrow staircase. Thumps and bumps and instructions sounded down through the floor. Simon went as if to follow up the stairs. Abigail grabbed him. 'Hold him, would you,' she said to Charity, 'while I find him something to eat.'

Charity dropped her bundle and received him awkwardly on her knee, uncertain how to restrain him. He struggled and protested. What did one do with unknown little children? She tried to hum a tune she knew, but he wasn't to be mollified.

'He has contended with so many new people in the last few weeks,' Abigail said, taking him back and feeding him fingers of bread.

'That's done!' Thomas emerged from the stairway. 'Hal is just lacing the ropes. He'll bring a mattress in a little while. I need to get back to the Tanyard.'

Abigail followed him to the street door, whispering 'Who is she? Where is she from? Why is she here?'

'I'll tell you by and bye,' Thomas said, quietly but not so quietly that Charity did not pick up what he said. 'She'll help you in the house – she knows how to do that. Just be gentle with her,' and he was gone.

The lad he had called Hal came back down. Simon toddled up to him, brandishing a crust. Hal squatted at his level. 'Is this for me, then?' and he tickled Simon and made him giggle. He looked up at Charity. 'He's a sort of little brother,' he said.

He almost collided in the doorway with another tall man coming in, a man older than Thomas, at first glance a handsome man. But when he turned, Charity saw that one side of his face was deeply scarred and distorted. He exchanged a word or two with Hal, then came right in and kissed Abigail. The soldier husband! He must be the soldier! Charity shrank into herself.

'Ralph, this is Charity,' Abigail said. 'Tom brought her this afternoon, and I think she is to stay with us for a while.'

Ralph held out his hand as if to shake hers, but Charity slipped off the stool and just dropped a small curtsey. She wanted to run, as she would have done at home when strange men came, new labourers taken on for the farm or beggars at the door, if only now there was somewhere to run to.

'We don't know anything about her.'

They had gone to bed while there was still light in the May sky. Abigail lay awake, staring at nothing. Charity had crept upstairs as if unwillingly, to the little back room that Abigail had destined for Hal.

'M'mm?' Ralph said, half asleep.

'Charity, Ralph. We know nothing about her. Except that she's an orphan.'

Abigail turned on her side, facing Ralph. 'Tom keeps rushing off, like he did at Wallingford. All he said was 'I've brought you an orphan.' Who is she? Where does she come from? And why has he brought her?'

'You brought Hal to the Tanyard when his mother had died and you found him,' Ralph murmured.

'That was different. Just down the road. And he had no one.'

'Maybe Charity has no one,' Ralph said.

'She's like a scared rabbit, all eyes and never a word.'

'This isn't like you, sweetheart,' Ralph said, touching her lightly.

'It's just… all our plans… everything seemed to be falling into place. Back in Farnham, a house, a place for us to work, a home to make for Hal, and then this. An unknown girl landed on us, and we'll have to take care of her, and find her something to do, and get Simon used to her, and… and we won't be able to have Hal living with us, will we.'

'Abigail!' Ralph said, drawing her close. 'If I obtain an apprenticeship for Hal, he'll be living away. He's not a child any more.' She could feel him smile in the dusk. 'You might like to have a daughter.'

'Is that what Tom means her to be? Or a servant?' Ralph said nothing. 'I so wanted Hal to be with us. You loved him too!'

'It's because I care for him that I'm looking on the long term. Once he's qualified at his trade he can be with us, a real partnership.'

'Seven years. Seven years apprenticeship.'

'Maybe longer,' Ralph said. 'I've been round the saddlers and horse-collar makers, and they've all got apprentices, won't take on another for a while.'

'Is that where you were all day? Oh Ralph!' She moved over

to him, burrowing her head into the crook of his arm, and he held her to him.

Charity, lying awake in the bare little room, could hear the murmur of voices through the studding wall, unsure whether this was reassuring or frightening. Hal had laced the rope well onto the wooden bed frame, but the flock-filled mattress was lumpy. Her grandmother would have brought it outdoors, had the cover unpicked and the lumps of woollen waste teased out. You did what Grandmother commanded.

Thomas. Whenever she had recoiled in fear from men, she had found comfort in the thought of Thomas. Nameless, and faceless too for she could not properly recall how he had looked, he was the wrestler who had saved her life. But now it was as if that thought were no more than a myth. He was just an ordinary man, who had done what Grandmother had told him to do, and brought her to this disordered household, and left her here. It seemed that he was concerned only to get her off his hands and into those of his sister.

How could she possibly know whom to trust?

For these last days, Charity's coming had dominated Thomas' thinking. Now, with Charity received by Abigail, and with Margie and Ned fed and bedded at Tanyard House and sent on their way, he turned his attention back to his trade.

He went to the stable where Hal was grooming the horses. Hal looked up at his cheery 'Good morrow!' but said nothing.

'Hired horses are all very well,' Thomas said, 'but I'm glad to be back with my old friends.' He patted Blaze. 'Behaved well on the way from Wallingford?'

Hal nodded.

Thomas wandered over to pick up the notebook where he scribbled his carting commitments. 'Oh no! We've missed a good one – that load of gunpowder from Chilworth.'

Hal muttered, 'I did it.'

'What, on your own? .

Hal muttered something into the mane he was teasing out.

'Did you?' Thomas asked. Hal might be taciturn but when he spoke it was normally direct and audible. 'Come on Hal, let's hear about it.'

Hal detached himself from the grooming and came over to Thomas. They were much the same height, eyes on a level, but he seemed reluctant to face up to him. 'I got help,' he said.

'Not Ralph?' Thomas asked.

Hal shook his head. Then taking a deep breath he straightened up and looked at Thomas squarely. 'I took Abe Trussler.'

'Abe? You took Abe Trussler?'

Hal nodded.

'Good God! That rogue! Whatever possessed you? You always said he hated you.'

'I needed someone. And he knows carting.'

'You didn't pay him did you?'

'I gave him a third of what I was paid,' Hal admitted. Then seeing Tom's expression he added, 'Wasn't that the just thing to do?'

'Well. Yes. I suppose it was, seeing he was sharing the work. Except that I wouldn't pay an assistant that much. How was he with our horses?'

'I drove them mostly.'

'That's as well. He doesn't treat his horses kindly.'

'I think,' Hal said, 'he was surprised at how they respond to commands.'

Thomas laid a hand on Star's neck, rubbing her gently. 'But Hal,' he said, 'Abe's up to no good. He'll do some dirty trick on you any time. He hates all Mannorys.'

'He called me "bastard Mannory",' Hal said. Then he grinned. 'And that is what I am! Except that if what Abigail says is true, I shall be an Attfield son.'

Thomas refused to be deflected. 'I don't see any good coming from associating with Abe. My father has always avoided conflict with him, but he has a terrible reputation.'

'His yard's a mess. His cart needs mending. He coughs,' Hal said.

'Judgment on the wicked, I'd say,' Thomas said.

Hal turned to put the brush and currycomb on the shelf where they belonged. He took a while to say anything more. When he did, it was to murmur something about Mother Metcalfe and overcoming evil with good.

'It's bricks again, Hal,' Thomas said a few days later. 'I've to go into Hampshire for grain, so you had best take the small cart and the cob.'

Hal grunted. As usual at the end of the day's work they were in the stable attending to the horses.

'You know the weight of bricks the cart can take,' Thomas said. 'The brakes are in order, for coming down the steep hill past the castle.'

'Where are the bricks to go?' Hal asked.

'Just beyond the town bar, in East Street. Everyone seems to be building now that we're clear of the fighting.'

'Everyone?' Hal asked.

'Figgs, father and son, in this case. More hop kilns.'

Thomas started plaiting Blaze's tail, weaving in a bright red ribbon. Loving his pair of horses as he did, he took pleasure in their adornment. Hal had finished grooming and seemed to be looking about for something else to do.

'So you'll do the brick load tomorrow,' Thomas said.

'Tom…' Hal said. 'I… took Abe Trussler's broken wheel to Moth in the wagon yard, and now he's mended it. Once we're down Castle Hill we could add a bit to the cart load, it's fairly level going along East Street, could I…?'

'Could you what?'

'Could I take the wheel along to Abe's yard?'

Thomas dropped the half finished plait, put his hands on his hips and regarded Hal, a mixture of emotions on his face.

'What's this with you and Abe?'

Hal said nothing.

'What's in it for you?'

Hal picked up Blaze's tail and started to continue the plait.

'Leave that!' Thomas knocked his hands aside. 'Answer me! Why do you keep getting mixed up with Abe Trussler?'

'It's just… his cart is no good to him without this wheel.'

'So?'

'So he can't earn. Not with the carting side of his business.' Hal pulled his shoulders back and stood tall. 'I know you mistrust him and all that, but the man has to eat.'

'You can put a pole through the axle hole and walk it along if that's what you want,' Thomas said at last. 'I'll not let Figg think I'm taking advantage of his order.'

In his shed in the wagon yard Moth, a little man with big hands, looked up from the spokes he was fitting into a new wheel. Abe's wheel leant up against the shed doorway, its rim chest high.

'Walking it?' he said. 'That's a rare one! All through the town?'

Hal nodded. He had cut a smooth ash pole and held it ready.

'Why you doing that?' Moth said.

Hal stood there silently, holding his pole. Thomas was good to work with. In all the time he had worked as his assistant, Thomas had never shown a harsh side like this. Surely it could not be wrong to give a hand to someone in need of help. Yet Thomas had this hatred of Abe.

'Why you doing that?' Moth asked again.

'I just have to,' Hal said.

Moth scratched his head. 'You'll need someone t'other side of the wheel.' Hal had not thought of that. 'Can't have it running away from you, knocking folk down.'

'Hey, Isaac!' he called to a lad at the back of the shed. 'Here's a laugh for you! Always one for a joke,' he added to Hal.

Isaac, a strapping lad much the same age as Hal, set up the contrivance with him and they started up Snow Hill, the wheel wobbling in the sandy surface, the pair of them holding fast to either end of the pole. At each wobble, Isaac laughed, so that by the time they reached the top of the steepest part of the hill they were both laughing and had to pause to recover their breath.

Passers by stopped and commented.

'This some new clown act?'

'Where you going? London town?'

'Heave ho! Let's see it roll!'

Hal and Isaac started off again, easier now on the firmer road surface, through the Borough, past the town bar, and on along beside Figg's building site, attracting children and young men calling encouragement as they went.

So it was quite a crowd which came to a halt outside Trussler's yard. Hal stood by the entrance, steadying the wheel.

A couple of men who were shifting suspended hides from one pit to another, looked up at the noise. Abe erupted out of a shed.

He looked aghast for just a moment. Then he was on to Hal, furious. "What's this riot? Go away! Get out!'

The crowd was wavering, half drawing back. Isaac was laughing again.

'A joke is it? You can get out of here, the lot of you! Get out!'

'Mister Trussler,' Hal said quietly, 'I've brought your wheel. It's mended.'

It was as if Abe hadn't noticed the wheel, only the crowd.

No one moved. The supporting crowd stood still. Abe's men looked on sheepishly. Abe surveyed the wheel.

Finally Hal said 'We'll bring it in, shall we?' and without waiting for an answer he and Isaac trundled it down to where the cart lay, still unusable. They pulled the pole out of the axle hole and turned to go.

'You'll need to pay Moth,' Hal said as he passed Abe.

The crowd escorted them back into the town, cheerful at Abe Trussler's humiliation, thinning out as they went.

Chapter 6 - Ann and James

Ann Gary surveyed the table and her brother Robert. 'Is this all your stuff?'

Robert looked up. 'It's what I've found in the Park.'

'Why have you spread it all over the table? Mother won't be pleased with these iron things on the polish we take so much trouble over.'

'Don't worry, I set them out carefully. I'm putting like with like. Maybe I'll make some boxes to keep them separate.'

Ann sat down. She had nothing much to do. 'What are these great heavy balls?'

'Cannon balls. Eight pound they weigh. James Mannory says they were fired by demi-culverin cannons right there behind the Castle, when the Royalists attacked from Odiham.'

'How does he know that?' Ann asked.

'He was there!'

Ann rolled the cannon ball idly to and fro.

'Heavy, isn't it,' Robert said. 'It takes six pounds of black powder to fire it. And the cannon itself is over eleven feet long. They need strong horses to move them.'

He pointed out a cluster of small balls. 'This small shot comes from the muskets, though James says not many were fired that day. I've mostly found them after the militia's firing practice.'

Ann picked up something about the size of an apple and turned it around in her hand.

'I've only one of those,' Robert said. 'James says it must

have been dropped accidentally, because it was for the portable leather guns and they weren't fired until the battle of Alton, ten miles away.'

'I suppose James was there as well.'

Robert hardly noticed Ann's resigned tone.

'Oh yes!' he said. 'With the London Auxiliaries. When they were in London he was a sergeant of ordnance and collected weaponry from the Tower. He knows it all.'

'He knows all about tanning too,' Ann said, a little wearily. The way she said it diverted Robert's attention from his collection.

With the directness of a young brother he said 'You're going to marry him aren't you?' Ann did not reply, still turning the ball in her hands. 'He's here often enough. And takes you out. And keeps gazing at you. So are you going to marry him?'

Ann stirred in her seat and replaced the cannon ball. 'Probably,' she said.

'Do you like him?'

She did not reply at once. Then she said, as if totting up on her fingers, 'He's a good match. Sturdy. And quite good looking.'

'And?' prompted Robert.

'He has a profitable trade. He talks of expanding that. And,' she added, 'he says he's found a cottage to rent, just right, in Church Lane.'

'But do you like him?'

She took a while to reply. For all the mundane conversations they had had on various walks, for all the hours she had listened to James explaining tanning, and musketry, and politics, there was that exchange of looks that very first day, which had stirred a gut attraction.

'Well. Yes,' she said. 'I suppose I do.'

Michael and Betty Gary quite evidently approved of James as a husband for Ann. He had become familiar with the family, and spent many hours with Ann herself. Yet still he hesitated. She seemed to listen attentively to all he said, albeit passively, and he longed for the spark which had drawn him to her at the start.

Now he had found this cottage to rent, a small one close to the baker in Church Lane, a good place to start married life; not far from her mother, or from his own mother just across the river for support and guidance, and within easy reach of his daily work.

'Come!' he said, one Sunday afternoon, 'Come and see the little house I'd like to rent.' The landlord had given him the key.

He had to stoop slightly to go through the doorway from the lane, stepping at once into a small square room. A fireplace was centred in the opposite wall with a cupboard to one side, but apart from those fixtures it was empty.

Ann stood quite still, looking about her.

'There's space to stack faggots of wood beside the hearth,' James said, 'And look, there's a cupboard under the stairs.'

'It needs a table,' she said, 'and stools and things.'

James mentally calculated how much floor space these would occupy. It would have to be a small table.

A staircase curled up in one corner and they had to duck to go under it and through to the back room. Smaller than the first room, a few shelves stood along one wall above a big wooden sink.

'Perhaps a work table could go in here,' James said.

'What about water?' Ann asked

'The pump house is just round the corner,' James said.

Outside the back door, wooden bins held wood and some coal, and beyond was what might be called a garden. 'You could keep hens here,' Ann said.

They went back indoors. 'No parlour,' Ann said.

'Let's look upstairs.' James led the way to where one room occupied the whole area under the roof rafters. And there was a bed. Just the frame and the rope lattice laced across it. No mattress, but the rope criss-crossing the frame looked sound and taut, and there was the structure needed for bed curtains and a cover over the head. Even without drapery or mattress, it looked inviting.

Ann bent down and tested the rope. Then she sat down on the bed and bounced a little. A glimmer of a smile. James sat down beside her. Her hands lay together in her lap. He took them both in his. The smile faded, but she looked right into his eyes, as if into his soul; the look that churned him up; the look that stirred his desires; the look that took control of him, aroused him as surely it must be arousing her.

He pulled her into his arms, tight close to his body, and she yielded deliciously. He pushed back her cap to feel her hair, kissing all over her face. His mouth sought hers. He filled it with his own, until at last she pulled away and he collected himself.

'Ann! Ann, could you marry me,' he panted, 'even in this cottage? It won't always be thus, I'll find a better house, I promise you.' He searched her face. 'Say you will, Ann. Say you'll be my wife.'

'Of course I will,' she said.

Betty Gary counted her family out of the house like so many chickens out of the hen house. Her husband left early with Christopher, before the counting started, and John tried to avoid her by being away to the shop soon after them. Robert, lazy fifteen year-old, she shoo'ed to the shop despite his protests, after which Nathanial and George had to be rounded up for school. This left little Michael, her pet lamb, and the girls.

'Into the parlour with you!' she said, 'and mind you do what Ann says and apply yourselves to your sewing.'

She closed the street door. Michael could go out later and play with neighbouring children, though she often complained, wishing that some of them were not of the rougher sort. She went back into the kitchen where the servant girl was cleaning the fireplace.

'Oh, Ann!' she called. Ann came. 'Ann, that Abigail is back in Farnham, along with the horse dealer she went off with. Some girl has gone to live with them, brought there it is said by Thomas Mannory. No one has seen her. Very strange. I think we should take a little gift along, a sort of welcome. Would you do that?'

She started inspecting her store cupboard. With winter stocks near depleted and summer crops yet to come, May was the hungry gap. 'What can we spare?' she said.

'Your hens have started laying.' The daily collection of eggs was Ann's task.

'That would do well. I'll put a few in one of the rush baskets the girls were making. There. And find out all you can!'

'Where are they living?'

'Goodness me! I thought everyone knew by now! That house that's been empty a while, just opposite the top of Snow Hill.'

'It's raining,' Ann said.

'Come! You only have to cross West Street!'

Ann knocked cautiously at the door she hoped was the right one. A man with a battered face came. The door opened straight into a room where a bench was strewn with strips of leather. The woman sitting there looked up. Abigail of course!

'Ann!' She hastened over to greet her. 'Come in!'

Ann held out the rush basket. 'Mother sent you these eggs.'

'That is kind of her. Come through into the kitchen so I can put them somewhere safe.' Abigail led into the back room where a young girl was peeling onions, a dainty girl with small features.

'Charity,' Abigail said, 'This is Ann Gary. I've know her since she was little.' She put the basket on a shelf. 'Ann is one of a big family. How many are you now, Ann?'

'Still the same,' Ann said. 'Nine of us. And Joan too.'

'No baby yet?'

Ann shook her head.

'Why don't you stay and chat to Charity? She doesn't know anyone here yet. I need to keep an eye on little Simon while we work.'

Ann sat down on a stool and looked round the room. All it had was a table and a few stools, shelves on one wall and a cupboard of sorts beside the chimney breast.

It was Charity who broke the silence. 'Nine children?' she said.

'Not all children,' Ann said. 'The older boys work in the shop with Father. And Christopher's about to have a baby – I mean his wife is.'

Charity giggled.

'Mother is eager to have a grandchild. She'll probably take charge of the baby, now she's past child-bearing. I shouldn't be surprised if Joan will wonder whose baby it really is.'

'Do you all live in one house?' Charity asked.

'Yes. It's quite big but it is crowded, and Christopher and Joan have this enormous bed which was bequeathed to Christopher and which takes up one whole room. Christopher talks of finding a house of their own.'

She paused. Those onions must have been kept all winter, they had so many rotten layers. Charity was discarding the bad into a leather bucket, piling on the table what was left that was good.

'And I'm to be married soon, so that will be one less in the house.'

Charity picked up the last of the onions and chopped off its top and the tough root end.

'In fact,' Ann said, 'I'm marrying Abigail's brother James. He's the best tanner in Farnham. He works with his father in the big tannery across the river.'

Charity finished peeling the last onion and began to chop the ones she had saved, as Abigail had asked her to do.

'We won't have to live at the tannery of course,' Ann said. 'James has found a little house right near the bakery by the church, and that will serve until the babes start to come.' She shifted her stool back a little. 'Chopping onions usually makes people cry,' she said.

'Not when they've been kept all winter long. Don't you find that?'

'Oh, I don't normally have anything to do with the cooking,'

Ann said. 'We employ a cook and a servant girl. They come in daily. And Mother is famous for her plum cake.'

Charity scraped the onion pieces into an iron pot and put on the lid. She turned her attention to a few carrots which had survived the winter in a clamp and were beginning to sprout.

A thought struck Ann. 'Are you employed as cook?' she asked. Charity shook her head. She had welcomed the task of preparing vegetables, a reminder of home, of her grandmother, a strange sort of comfort.

'I'd rather sew,' Ann said. 'I have to supervise my sisters and check their stitching.' She went on to explain what they were making and how, and how long she supposed they would take to complete their current work, and whether they would help make her wedding garments if their stitches were neat enough. And what she would choose from her father's stock of woollen cloth, and whether they could afford lace on her shift, and when they could start on the dressmaking.

Abigail came through carrying Simon. 'Have you a little stick of carrot there? Simon likes to chew it and it helps his teething.'

Ann stood up to take her leave. 'I'll see you again, Charity. I don't often have the chance of a new friend.'

Betty Gary greeted her home with, 'Well. That must have been a good chat you had. What did you find out?'

'Her name's Charity,' Ann said.

'And?'

'She was chopping vegetables.'

'She's their cook then?'

Ann shook her head as Charity had done.

'Well! Much use you are! Small return for a basket of eggs!'

'Eat with us when you can,' Abigail had said, and today was the first opportunity Hal had found. He had tended the horses, hitched the small cart for Thomas to take to the forest for fresh spring oak bark for tanning, cleaned the stable, and run through the sudden rain to the house. A goodly smell greeted him as he went in.

'Food, or leatherwork?' Ralph laughed.

'Which comes first?' Hal said.

'We've made good progress with work this morning,' Abigail said. 'I asked Charity to prepare vegetables, and she lit the fire and scraped the bacon and had it all simmering before I realised. So we'll be eating soon.'

Ralph handed him an already stitched strap. 'Can you attach this to the metal ring?' He watched as Hal worked, his fingers deft and strong. 'You haven't lost your skill,' he said.

'There's often repairs to do on our harness,' Hal said, then corrected himself. 'Tom's harness.'

Abigail looked at him sharply. 'Tom…?'

Hal said nothing.

Ralph said 'I'm sorry to say I've not succeeded in finding a horse-collar maker to take you as an apprentice. In Farnham that is. I suppose I could try further afield. Even Petersfield. I'll need to go to Petersfield some time soon, to see what's left of my inheritance there. Only a field or two.'

He idly turned over some leather scraps, piling them almost without looking. 'All those places where I used to collect horses for sale.' He sounded wistful.

'Horses,' Hal said.

Simon toddled over and attached himself to his leg.

'Hullo you!' Hal said.

'Up!' Simon said. Then he saw that the door into the back room was opening, bringing with it an appetising smell. He headed instantly towards it.

'I think the bacon is cooked now,' Charity said. She had laid bowls on the table, drawn ale and cut bread. She had even found a dish for the bacon, which Ralph proceeded to carve. Once everyone was settled, Simon on Abigail's lap, he returned to the topic still on his mind.

'There must be collar-makers in all those villages around Petersfield,' he said. 'I could hire a horse and go along that way.'

'Or eastward, Guildford and so on,' Abigail said. 'But Hal, these years since you and Ralph learnt harness making with Mother Metcalfe, these years that you've been back here, what has occupied you?'

'Tom's horses,' Hal said.

Ralph looked at him long and hard. 'That's your love, isn't it,' he said. 'And,' as he mopped the last of the juices out of his plate with a hunk of bread, 'your gift, your special gift.'

'You so want Hal to be a partner with you in business,' Abigail said.

'Maybe this is a sign that I shouldn't pursue the idea,' Ralph said.

Hal speared a last piece of bacon on his knife. 'Tom's not pleased with me at present,' he said, but he did not elaborate.

Abigail transferred Simon from her own lap to Ralph's. 'I'll wash the bowls and tankards while the kettle is still warm from the embers,' she said. 'Hal, we need a loaf. On your way back to the Tanyard, would you show Charity where the baker is?'

Momentarily that look of a scared rabbit shut in Charity's face. To the baker, alone, with Hal? But Abigail was giving her coins. As ever, the decision was made for her, there was no escape.

Hal was a cheerful, if silent, companion. Rain had left the cobbled road shining and puddled. Jumping over patches of water, he looked to Charity to do the same. She did her best, despite the impediment of her skirt. Then she misjudged and landed one foot squarely in a puddle.

'Oh, sorry!' Hal said. 'I forgot you're not a boy.'

'I don't mind being treated as one,' Charity found herself saying.

Hal slowed his pace and led round Church Lane.

'The baker's there by the corner,' he said. 'See the big bread oven in its wall?' He paused at the bakery door. 'I'll nip through between the houses and go across the wagon yard.' He laughed. 'I've a friend there. We were on a proper caper the other day. Gathered quite a crowd. Got me into more trouble though.' He laughed again and was gone.

Chapter 7 - London and Farnham

Thomas bounded into Tanyard House eager to tell his news to anyone who would listen. The house seemed deserted. Then he heard a small sound from beyond the chimney stack, his mother Phoebe tidying the bake room. She heard him.

'Tom! You're back early!'

'Mother, look! A contract! I'm contracted to deliver grain and flour to London from the mills here in Farnham. Every week, Mother!'

'Dear Tom!' His mother embraced him. 'What a blessing!'

'Regular, every week, and not hanging about looking for the next job. I couldn't ask for better. Piggott the corn chandler arranged it, all properly drawn up and signed!' He looked lovingly at the paper in his hand. 'I must lodge it safely.'

By evening all the household knew the news.

'London?' James said. 'I've skins I'd like to get to London. You could carry those along with the meal.'

'Where do they have to go?' Thomas sounded doubtful.

'You could deliver them to Kiffin's house until we make a more permanent arrangement. And there's Finsbury stables close by where you could lodge the horses overnight.'

'I'll need to buy another tarpaulin somewhere,' Thomas said.

His father was less enthusiastic. 'The tannery is becoming over crowded, with business that has nothing to do with tanning. Three horses you have now, and your big wagon lodged wherever you find a corner. Where do you propose to store the grain between your journeys to London?'

But Thomas had forestalled him, thinking and planning and negotiating on his way back from Piggott, contract in hand. 'There's that granary just across the river, on the town side of the long bridge,' he said. 'I've talked with Mills who owns it, and he may be prepared to come to some arrangement. He has stabling there too, which he is scarcely using, and it backs onto the wagon yard, where the wagons come in with the grain. I'll need to clear it with Piggott of course.'

'As corn chandler he will certainly have his own opinion on the matter,' Jacob said.

Out in the shed cleaning the tack that evening, an unexpected aspect of this contract struck Thomas.

'When I'm in London,' he said to Hal, 'I'll need you to look after the business here. Carting with the small cart and the cob, and noting down orders.'

Hal nodded, saying nothing.

'And mind you carry on just as I do,' Tom added. 'No messing about with damn Trussler.'

When Hal made no response, simply wiping harness and hanging it up, Tom repeated 'No messing, I said. No messing with Abe Trussler.'

Hal faced him. 'The Master,' he said. 'He's spoken sometimes about a feud Abe Trussler has with the Mannory family.'

'That's Trussler's concern, resenting something done to his father by my grandfather. My father has always refused to enter into it, but Abe keeps up his hatred.'

Hal said quietly 'So this is a new feud?'

The rain held off the day in June that Thomas set out, and

he covered the miles to London without trouble. At a ship's chandler between the road and the river Thames, having given a lad a tip to mind the horses and the load, he managed to buy a new tarpaulin. He delivered the sacks of flour to the granary Piggott has listed, then headed up through the City walls to the Finsbury stables, grateful for James' knowledge of London. He decided to leave the skins at the stables until he had made himself and his errand known.

He was readily directed to the Kiffins' pleasant house. It stood just outside the City Walls where Moorgate gave access to Moorfields. His tentative knock at the door was quickly answered.

'Master Kiffin?' Thomas said.

'I am he. What is your errand?'

'I've brought skins from James Mannory. I'm his brother Thomas.'

'Skins eh? Where are they?'

'I've left them at Finsbury stables where I've lodged my horse and cart.'

'Who is it, Will?' A woman's voice from within the house.

'You'd best come in,' Kiffin said. He led the way into the parlour. 'My wife Hanna.'

'We thought you may have come with news from the Army,' Hanna said. They sat down and poured ale. 'The servants are already abed,' she said.

'Perhaps I should explain the situation you find us in,' Kiffin said. 'You know the Army is gathered at Newmarket, and the regiments there have each elected an adjutator, like a representative, an agent. General Fairfax has his eye on them. One or two usually ride into the City each day to exchange news, lodging overnight in various houses. We were expecting one this evening, to lodge here.'

'Whoever it is to be, is late tonight,' Hanna said.

'I wish my brother James were here,' Thomas said.

'James?' William Kiffin chuckled. 'Always passionate for equality and justice, though uncertain how either could be achieved. Well, you'll be able to take him the latest news.'

He leapt up as another knock came at the door, and admitted a weather-beaten man, somewhat older than Thomas.

'Philip!' Kiffin said. 'Welcome!'

Philip settled himself down to take the proffered refreshment.

'Tell us what has been happening,' Hanna said.

'Where to begin?' Philip chewed thoughtfully and sipped his ale. 'The King was at Holmby House, up in the Midlands – remember? Last week a troop of cavalry went there, and after a few days, persuaded him to come away with them.'

'Who told them to do that?' William asked.

'Some say they did it on their own initiative. Some say General Cromwell had something to do with it, to get the King within reach. They brought him down to the Army at Newmarket.'

'As a prisoner?' Hanna said

'He was a prisoner of sorts at Holmby House – I mean, he wasn't at liberty to leave it. It seems General Fairfax and General Cromwell asked him if he would return there, but I understand he said he'd prefer to stay with the Army – something about the air at Newmarket suiting him better.'

'At least he has that choice,' Hanna said.

'More like he prefers to be where the action is. All the Army wants is its arrears of pay,' Kiffin said.

'And acceptable conditions too,' Philip said.

'I read the proposals and counter proposals,' Kiffin said. 'They lose no time printing and publishing them.'

'Commissioners from Parliament keep going back and forth,' Philip said. 'It drags on. Now all officers are to return to their regiments.' He drained his goblet and held it out for more.

'There are so many complications,' William said. 'You remember a month or so ago Parliament gave over control of the London Trained Bands to the City. Their Militia Committee is all Presbyterians, with Independents actually excluded. The Army is full of Independents, so it seems the City wants to arm themselves against the Army.'

Hanna shook her head. 'I don't understand why opinions about church leadership put people into such opposition.'

'One may wonder,' William said, 'what there is to choose between them. As John Milton has written, "New Presbyter is but old Priest write large". Those who go by the name of Independents want freedom of conscience as we do, freedom to believe and worship as they see fit without external control.'

'Differences of opinion don't have to lead to armed conflict,' Hanna said.

'But that is what is happening. The Common Council of the City is fearful because of the Army's refusal to be disbanded,' William said. 'They see it as a threat.'

'You know the simple things which we are asking,' Philip said. 'We don't want to ruin London. I'm told that General Fairfax and a dozen of his officers have written to the Lord Mayor to reassure the City of that.'

'The City is full of disturbance,' Kiffin said. 'Who can be

trusted? Who supports whom? Did you see Lilburne today?'

'I did,' Philip said. 'That's why I was late here. He said he has no more patience with petitions and politicking. His hope is with the Army.'

'Do you think he is right?' William asked

'Well, we have a Council of the Army now,' Philip said. 'Two commissioned officers and two private soldiers from each regiment along with the Generals, the Grandees. Some of the soldiers, like Edward Sexby, are most able men. Tomorrow all us soldiers are to have a day of fasting and humiliation to try to discern God's will. Officers too. Let's hope we hear truly.'

'We will pray too,' William Kiffin said.

Hanna stood up. 'We have a bed made up for you here if you wish to stay overnight. And,' turning to Thomas, 'you are welcome to stay too. You'll be wanting to do business with my husband in the morning I don't doubt.'

One quiet afternoon James stood beside the tanning pits, looking into them almost idly, for they had been checked that morning and nothing more was needed. It seemed that Jacob likewise did not have any pressing business, for he wandered through from the sheds and joined him. They stood silently for a while, satisfied that the tanning process was carrying on as it should do.

Then James took a deep breath. Such a moment might not recur.

'Father,' he said. 'You know Thomas has this weekly run to London. I got him to take some of the skins we have cured and Wilkins has curried, and deliver them to William Kiffin who is selling them for us. Kiffin is a Freeman of the Leathersellers'

Company, so he has useful contacts.'

Jacob grunted. 'Is selling, or has sold?'

'He already has the coupons for some that have been sold. He gets a far better price than we do selling to the glove-makers and cordwainers in Farnham.'

'You did not consult me about this. I take it that you pay Wilkins for his currying work, and then sell on the skins he has finished? And is the Tanyard to be paid as well? You should indeed have consulted me before you took this initiative.'

James swallowed. He had been afraid Jacob would find some objections to this new scheme of his. He stared away over the river to the meadows and the distant church tower. No use getting belligerent. This was too important. He must win his father round. He spoke unusually gently.

'Forgive me, Sir. Kiffin has a high opinion of the quality of the skins we produce. I have just wanted to test whether going through him was going to be profitable. You know I am keen to expand our work.'

Jacob moved away from the tanning pits, as if movement would aid thought.

'I see several problems,' he said at last. 'First of all, how to allocate the income secured from this possible London market; secondly, sourcing a greater quantity of skins.'

'I'm in touch with a fellmonger we've not used before....'

Jacob raised his hand. 'Then there is a matter of space. At present curing skins takes up little space in this yard and we need the pits for the big hides.'

James took a breath to answer, but Jacob went on, 'How much of your time would be taken up with trading? Is that compatible with your role as yard foreman?'

James looked at him in amazement. These were problems which could be worked out, if Jacob were behind him.

'Then would you support me in this project?' James dared to ask.

'Support?' Jacob looked round the yard with its flank of sheds, its rows of tanning pits. 'This tannery is my prime concern. I will not stand in your way so long as my business is not put at risk.'

James nodded, silently. Foreman he might be, but the business was still entirely his father's, under his control.

'I'm willing to discuss,' Jacob added, 'but you have to take responsibility for this plan of yours.'

'Thank you, Father.'

They stood together by the river, silent for a while. Then Jacob said, 'The Gary girl. What are your intentions there?'

'There's a cottage to rent, I've shown her, I'd like to marry her very soon.' James' words came out in a rush. Somehow he had imagined his father had not noticed his frequent visits to the Gary household, nor his watching Ann at church. But Phoebe, his mother, would have done so.

'What age are you now?'

'All but thirty,' James said.

Jacob grunted. 'Old enough I suppose. Another distraction from the Tannery'

'Oh… James opened his mouth to protest, but Jacob forestalled him.

'A good match,' he said, and turned away.

'Only a month !' Betty Gary exclaimed. She had propped the street door ajar and opened every window she could open and still the July heat penetrated the house. She sat spread in one of the chairs with the cushion thrown onto a bench, where her daughters sat dilatorily sewing.

'Only a month! Are they calling the banns already?'

'Next Sunday is the first,' Ann said.

'So three Sundays after that. What more time will James allow us?'

'He doesn't want to wait any longer than need be,' Ann said, and nor, if truth be told, did she.

'What will people say, if there is such haste?'

'They'll say what you tell them. You're the one who spreads gossip.'

Betty bristled. 'Ann!'

Elizabeth and Jane giggled.

'Now girls! Get on with your sewing!' She turned back to Ann. 'I suppose your James will want a room here.'

'I've told you. James has found a cottage to rent, right by the bakery.'

'What about furniture? And cooking pots? Cauldrons and skillets and trenchers and ladles and goblets and knives. And buckets and jugs. Where can it all be found?'

'James has bought a few things.'

'And bed sheets, and coverings. Hangings for the bed – do you even have a bed?' Each new thought made her more emphatic.

'There is a bed,' Ann said.

'And clothing for your wedding!' Another thought.

'The girls can leave the shirts they are making, and help,' Ann said.

'Their stitching is still not very even.'

'We'll ask Joan – hers is perfect.'

'She's all taken up with the baby.'

'Mother!' Ann stamped her foot. 'The girls can hem bed sheets, and blanket stitch around a warm covering. I'm going to see Father.'

She did not slam the door as she would have liked to do. Keeping as much in the shade as possible, she went up the road and across to Castle Street and the shop. Michael Gary was serving a customer and her brother Christopher was rolling up some bolts of cloth. She stood just inside the door, looking at the stacked shelves with their rolls of variously coloured cloth.

The customer greeted her. 'So you're to be married,' she said. How quickly news spread around this town! She nodded but would not be drawn to elaborate.

To her father she said, 'Please could we find some cloth for my wedding?'

Michael smiled at her, the daughter he enjoyed seeing pleasingly dressed, looking so like her mother when they themselves first married.

'Clothing for yourself, or for the marriage bed?'

Ann hesitated. It seemed strange to have her own father talking in terms of the marriage bed, the bed which had awakened such passion in both herself and James.

'Mother says we need bed sheets and a covering, and if we obtain those soon, the girls will be able to hem and bind them.'

Michael lifted down two or three rolls of cloth. 'You could have broadcloth. It's fine, and wide enough to cover you both. Or some local russet. That's well fulled and shrunk, and very warm.'

'I'd like the broadcloth, and that rich blue. Please measure out what you think we'll need.'

'For bed sheets you will have to go to Wroth the linen draper.'

'He's the best draper, is he? Abigail Mannory, as was, has taken the house next to his shop, but I expect you know that.'

'Joan will be the one to advise you about clothes for your wedding. Always so elegant.' Michael relished his daughter-in-law.

Christopher looked up and grinned.

'Shall we make a list?' Joan suggested, forgetting until she noticed her expression, that Ann could barely read or write. Then she hastened to say, 'It's simple enough, we can list it in our heads. Shall we go to Wroth's shop and see what he has?'

Joan knotted her shawl to make a little sling for her baby and they set off together. 'Linen for bed sheets, and Master Wroth will know just what to provide for your clothing. Fine cambric for shifts.'

'I have plenty of shifts,' Ann said.

'You should have a new one for your wedding, one at least. And petticoats – skirts – one of linen, and another of warmer cloth in case the day is cold. And a bodice of course. And a coat, or a cape – a cape is more fashionable. And then tissue for the bride veil, strong enough to hold sprigs of rosemary and soft enough to drape over your head and shoulders.'

They reached the shop, and 'Why! Charity!' Ann exclaimed. She turned to Joan. 'This is Charity, who is living with Abigail and Ralph. What are you buying, Charity?'

'Just some thread,' Charity said.

Joan smiled at her. 'I'm Ann's sister-in-law, and we're looking for fabric for her wedding garments. Do you sew much?'

'Yes,' Charity said, quietly.

'What are you sewing that needs more thread?' Joan asked.

'Some embroidery, for cuffs,' and she held out her arm, revealing the fine embroidery on the cuff of her shift.

'That's beautiful!' Ann exclaimed. 'I had been wondering whether we could manage some lace on collar and cuffs, but embroidered designs would be pretty, and easier to come by than lace. Charity, would you do some for me? We have only a month until the wedding.'

George Wroth cleared his throat. 'May I show you some fabric?'

They turned to business then, until the baby started to mew and Joan said she must hurry home to feed her. 'We'll cut out the collars and cuffs, and bring them to you, Charity, unless you would prefer to come and work in our house?' she said.

'Thank you, I'll work at home if you don't mind,' Charity said, mindful of the teaming household Ann had told her about.

'And we'll pay you, of course,' Ann said as they left the shop. This transaction gave her a sense of importance, a grown-up thing to do. It gave her, too, a sense of being a benefactress, for whatever Abigail had said, Charity seemed to be little more than a servant in that household. And she was certainly skilled with her needle.

Ann made her sisters sit down daily to hem the bed linen her father had bought for her, and to blanket stitch the wool coverlets from his shop. She and Joan sat with them, cutting out and then stitching the garments they had agreed were needed.

Here, around the parlour table, she was in charge.

Every other aspect of the wedding had Betty Gary perpetually busy, if not organising all concerned, then talking endlessly about it. She kept nipping down to the cottage to add some item she considered necessary, checking what was there, ensuring it accorded with her own good taste. After every visit she would complain 'It's so small!'

As for plans for the wedding day itself, her great worry was that there was scarcely enough space in her own house for the well-wishers she hoped would come to toast the bride and groom. She almost persuaded her husband to empty his shop by taking all his stock upstairs so that they could assemble there, until James informed her that he had negotiated with his cousin, the publican at the Bush Inn, for the Inn to be the celebration venue. Then everyone she met had to be told about it, for surely it redounded to their status in the town.

She found a large two-handled basket into which she folded the completed bedclothes. 'Nathaniel, George! Come and carry this for me!' She dared not trust them to the cottage alone, so she followed as they wove their way down the street, arguing as they went.

'Lift it up!' Nathaniel said. 'It's scraping the ground.'

'Lift it up yourself!' George retorted. 'You're taller'n me.'

'Hold it with both your hands.'

'Then I'll have to walk sideways.'

'Get on with you, do!' Betty said. 'Nathaniel, go on the left where the roadway slopes down.'

'I'll be in the gutter!' as they changed sides. Then George tripped and all but fell into the basket. He swung his legs round 'Oh! It's comfortable in here.'

Betty hauled him out. 'I don't know why I bother with you,' she said.

'Because we're strong!' Nathaniel flexed his muscles.

At last they arrived at the cottage. The boys had not been inside before, and charged about inspecting every corner. Upstairs, Betty had already hung the bed draperies, where the boys pretended to hide and leap out at each other.

'Out!' Betty commanded. She proceeded to make up the bed. Under it lurked an earthenware chamber pot. Her sons clattered down the stairs and erupted into the backyard where she had got their brother Robert to scythe the long grass.

The bed made, she rounded them up in her habitual manner. They ran home ahead of her, bursting in on the dressmaking scene, tranquil until that moment.

'Look Mother!' Ann said as Betty followed them indoors. 'Look at what Charity has made!' Collar and cuffs were beautifully embroidered. 'All we need to do now is to attach them to the shift.'

Charity stood quietly in one corner as her work was applauded. Betty looked at her as if for the first time. She could not but admire the skill and delicacy of her work. It was as if, to her, momentarily Charity had become a person, a person with a useful skill, rather than an inconsequential enigma.

So the clothing was ready, food prepared, the day set aside, and many townsfolk gave themselves time off work to attend the ceremony in the church. The Rector met the bride and groom at the entrance and asked them the questions prescribed in the Book of Common Prayer, a book now out of favour except for such occasions. For better, for worse, for richer, for poorer, in sickness and in health… to love, honour and (for

106

Ann) to obey; so they vowed. The bride veil was thrown back and everyone moved into the church for the sermon.

So much for the formalities. James endured these, the conviviality, the congratulations, the eating and drinking, becoming more and more desperate to have Ann in bed. The cottage being so small he managed to block the young men and women eager to crowd in and put them to bed. He hustled Ann up the stairs, she laughing as she went, and almost tore her clothes off her before flinging his own on the floor.

Their coupling was not the bliss they had anticipated. His haste gave her no comfort or caress. She cried out in pain, and there was blood.

Chapter 8 - Politics and Physick

Towards the end of July, William Kiffin came home from a meeting with his church elders, burdened with news from the City. He sat down disconsolately.

'I don't know what to make of it,' he said. 'It is as if, after all the fighting, the Army and the City are at war, and who knows where Parliament stands. Independents and Presbyterians vying for power. In fact eleven Presbyterian members of Parliament are banned from the House.'

'I tried to make some purchases today,' Hanna said, 'but the shops were shut. I heard drums beating all around.'

'They're trying to recruit to the Militia,' William said. 'The City Council has appointed two Generals, two soldiers of fortune. Massie and Poyntz. I'm wary of both from what I've heard.'

'Didn't General Massie prevent King Charles reaching allies in Scotland?'

'He did. I suppose I should not doubt him just because he's a convinced Presbyterian. Actually he's one of those members of Parliament who has been excluded from the House.'

'And Poyntz?' Hanna asked.

'He's been fighting all his life with one side or another. All over Germany. They say he had his successes for Parliament, but then his troops mutinied over pay, and took him to General Fairfax as their prisoner. That happened just weeks ago. The General released him at once, but didn't re-employ him.'

'So he went to London.'

'To raise troops. I wonder what success these Generals are having.'

'You say this is to oppose the Army?' Hanna said.

'The City Council demands that the Army stays thirty miles distant from the City. So far they have complied. If only Parliament would give them the pay they are owed, and meet some of their just conditions, I reckon they would willingly disband. It's not as if money can be short, with all the royalist properties that have been sequestered.'

'So it's City against Army and Army against Parliament.' Hanna said, and then almost in a whisper, 'William, if the City is enlisting troops and General Fairfax has his great Army not far off, shall we be under siege? We're outside the city walls here, so we wouldn't have the walls to protect us if the Army besieged the city.'

William looked at her speculatively. 'Would you prefer to take our daughter away from London? We could ask Thomas Mannory this evening if he could take you with him into the country.'

'Leaving you alone here? No indeed!' She moved over to him and embraced him, feeling the tension ease from his shoulders.

He smiled at her. 'I'd almost forgotten to tell you. A young gentleman has arrived from the New World, and I have invited him to eat with us tomorrow. He has a servant with him, who is seeking lodgings for them both. His name is John Woodbridge.'

He was a personable young man in his early thirties. His servant came with him, who seemed more like a friend than a servant, for he evidently expected to sit down at table with them.

Woodbridge was eager to explain their arrival.

'You must know of Hugh Peters the preacher.'

'Yes indeed,' William said. 'A very energetic man, and eloquent preacher. He is famous for urging on the Parliamentary Army's soldiers before battles in the late war, mixing high ideals with humour.'

'He was well liked in Massachusetts,' Woodbridge said, adding with a smile, 'at the church in Salem, once he had chased out those with whom he disagreed.'

'Their leaders had been exiled,' his servant said quietly.

'You heard about Anne Hutchinson?' Woodridge said. 'A gifted woman, who brought many women to faith and even some men. But she overreached herself, and the magistrates in Boston had her tried on various counts, and expelled her from the settlement.'

'They expelled Roger Williams too, didn't they,' William Kiffin said. 'I came to know him when he crossed back to England three or four years ago.'

'Roger Williams really does believe in freedom of conscience,' Woodbridge said, 'and the separation of church and state. He was firm that magistrates should not be empowered to condemn a person for what he believes. In God's providence he survived banishment and built up a good settlement. Rhode Island they called it. Persecuted believers have taken refuge there.'

'We spoke many times when he was in London,' William said. 'We agreed that baptism should be for believers, not for infants, and he did worship with us, but he was reluctant to be part of a particular church. A clever, generous-hearted man. But what of Hugh Peters?'

Woodbridge applied himself to the meat that Hanna had served him. 'This is very good if I may say so. Fish is still our main diet in the New World.'

'Hugh Peters?' William asked.

'Ah yes. I had to do with him in Massachusetts when I myself was ordained to preach. In the town originally called Chochichawicke, but we called it Andover after the Andover in Hampshire. So many of the names link us to the Old World.'

'But Peters has been back in England for some years now,' William said.

'Oh yes, all through the late war,' Woodbridge said. 'Peters is still much concerned with politics.' He sat back goblet in hand, at last coming to the point. 'You must know of all the discussion going on between different parties, and negotiations with the King. Peters is a renowned negotiator, mediator. But because he has been associated with the Parliamentary Army in many of its victories, he would not be acceptable to the King. Knowing that I have no particular affiliations, Peters recommended me to be chaplain to those who may attempt to negotiate with His Majesty.'

'Calling on the New World to help the Old,' Hanna said.

'We hear of such meetings from time to time,' William said. 'None seem to arrive at a definite conclusion.'

'I confess that I have yet to be called upon to take up the duties of chaplain,' Woodbridge said.

William refilled his goblet. Hanna replenished her daughter's plate. Lydia looked across the table at him. 'What do you do then?' she said. 'My papa is a merchant.'

Woodbridge smiled. 'I have a personal matter I am trying

to pursue. My sister-in-law is a most accomplished poet, and my intention is to find patrons to support the publication of her verse while I am in England.'

His servant broke in. 'The poems are absorbing,' he said. 'We read them during the calmer days of our voyage.'

'Will you read them to me?' Lydia asked.

'A task for you, Walter,' Woodbridge laughed.

'Some are quite long,' Walter said. 'Ancient history in verse; The Four Monarchies, Assyrian, Persian, Greek and Roman, although the Roman is not complete.'

'Anne Bradstreet the poetess, my sister-in-law,' Woodbridge said, 'often suffered illness, and she must have been dissatisfied with the drafts of the Roman monarchy, for she recorded that they were burnt.'

'Lydia would enjoy hearing that versified history,' Hanna said.

'I do not always have the manuscripts to hand,' Woodbridge said. 'Those whose literary patronage I am seeking often keep them longer than I would wish.'

John Woodbridge and Walter Hutchcroft soon became regular visitors to the Kiffins' house, sometimes armed with a portion of verse which delighted Lydia. Out at Moorfields they could, for a while, forget the tensions in the City.

'Here is a piece to interest you,' John Woodbridge said one warm day in August when Thomas was there. 'Let me read it to you. The Persian tyrant had died childless, and a new ruler was needed. The seven "satraps", as the provincial governors were called, discuss.'

All things in peace, the rebels thoroughly quelled,
A consultation by those states was held,
What form of government now to erect
The old, or new, which best, in what respect.
The greater part declined a monarchy
So late crushed by their prince's tyranny,
And thought the people would more happy be,
If governed by an aristocracy;
But others thought (none of the dullest brain)
That better one than many tyrants reign.
What arguments they used, I know not well,
Too politic, it's like, for me to tell,
But in conclusion they all agree,
Out of the seven a monarch chosen be.

'How little changes over the years!' William said. 'How is it in the New World?'

'Not exactly the freedom we emigrants hoped for,' Woodbridge said. 'The temptation to take control remains, wherever you are, and the wish to defend each one's understanding of the truth. From what I hear, the likes of John Lilburne promote a greater degree of democracy than we, in the New World, have so far achieved.'

'How did those Persians choose the monarch?' Lydia asked, waiting eagerly.

'Listen to the next stanza and you will hear,' Walter said. He took over the reading.

All envy to avoid, this was thought on,
Upon a green to meet by rising sun,

And he whose horse before the rest should neigh,
Of all the peers should have precedency.
They all attend on the appointed hour,
Praying to fortune for a kingly power.
Then mounting on their snorting coursers proud.
Darius' lusty stallion neighed full loud.
The nobles all alight, bow to their king
And joyful acclamations shrill they ring.
A thousand times, "Long live the king," they cry,
"Let tyranny with dead Cambyses die";
Then all attend him to his royal room:
Thanks for all this to's crafty stable-groom.

Thomas was the first to laugh. 'Hal would love that,' he said. 'The crafty stable groom.'

'Hal?' Lydia asked. 'Who is Hal?'

'My carting assistant, sort of half-brother. He has an understanding with horses.'

'Sort of half-brother,' Walter repeated. He looked at Lydia's eager face. 'I have a daughter somewhere,' he said. 'A few years older than you. I would dearly like to find her.'

General Poynz for the City militia was worsted by an Army troop in an encounter at Brentford. Fairfax and the bulk of the Army camped on Hounslow Heath, scarcely a day's march from the City. The City Councillors became ever more agitated and undecided, until finally they resolved to send Fairfax a letter, beseeching him that there might be a way of composure.

He met them in Kensington, where they offered humble submission. Supporters willingly opened the City gates, and the Army marched peaceably three abreast through Hyde Park into the City itself, one regiment circling to secure the river approaches. His twenty thousand soldiers headed for quarters in Croydon, whence they moved on to Putney.

King Charles and his retinue were moved to Hampton Court Palace.

Massie and Poynz fled to the Netherlands.

With Thomas away two days a week, Hal was often busy with the small cart, fulfilling his instructions. People going about their business around the town greeted him, and he began to notice the different levels of acknowledgement. Mr. Vernon, the only gentleman living in the town, expected hats to be doffed to him, although Hal had more than the ordinary relationship with him because the Vernons' groom, stable and horses had been his refuge as a child. When not on horseback, Mr. Vernon might stop and ask how he fared.

The town was run by the Burgesses, people like Michael Gary. They annually elected two Bailiffs from among their number. Everyone knew that George Wroth the present Bailiff was the one who had fined Abe Trussler for his poorly tanned hides.

Abe. Now Abe was a puzzle, whom no one seemed to trust and who was often ignored rather than greeted. Unlike most townspeople, other than servants and labourers, he had no particular trade but spread his interests around. He had inherited the Guildford Road tannery from past generations, a feckless tribe of whom many years ago the grandfather had come into conflict with the Mannorys.

He rented out several dilapidated houses in Abbey Street,

some of them occupied by women of doubtful reputation. He carted wherever need arose. He employed tannery workers, though he was an unpopular employer.

He seemed to have a particular hatred for Hal. Should their paths cross he was more likely to swear on some pretext than to greet. One such encounter occurred early in September.

Hal had had business which brought him back along Abbey Street, past the miserable hovel where he and his mother had lived until she died and Abigail found him and brought him to the Tanyard. It looked no better than it had in those days, shabby with a wonky roof which leaked after a storm. And Abe was standing in the alleyway beside it, standing still, and coughing. He looked up as Hal drove past, but anything he might have been inclined to say or shout was stifled by more coughing, much worse than when Hal had delivered the cart wheel.

A few days later, back in Tanyard House, Hal managed to speak with Phoebe alone. 'Mistress, would you have any physick to cure a cough?'

'A cough?' Phoebe said. 'You don't have a cough do you?'

'Not I, but someone I know,' Hal said.

Phoebe regarded him. She knew better than to question him. The lad always kept his own counsel, reluctant to divulge more than was strictly necessary. And it was none of her business who his sick friend might be.

'I have a decoction of horehound,' she said. 'It tastes unpleasant, but it does serve to relieve a cough.'

She went into the still room and reached down a little bottle from a high shelf. 'Just a small dose at intervals,' she said. 'It is not good to take too much.'

'Shall I pay you for it?' Hal said.

'Go on with you! It's my pleasure to use the plants God gives us for our good. May it bless your friend.'

Thomas set off for London early next morning. As Hal tended the little horse, he was beset with doubts. Thomas had told him so firmly not to mess with Abe. To take advantage of his absence to bring physick to Abe - that was disobedient, even deceitful. And the Bible said that servants should obey their masters, even the masters who were unreasonable. But the Bible also said we should be merciful – and heal the sick.

The only job Thomas had left him today was to take the next consignment of bricks to Figg's building site. He could do that this afternoon. There was not a great deal to do this morning, yet he kept spreading out the tasks. He led the horse out of the stable, through the wagon yard and into the meadows, leaving her hobbled to make sure she would be easy to catch later on. He went back through the wagon yard. He checked that all was correct in the stable, harness clean and oiled and hung up, floor swept and scrubbed, hay in the manger.

Finally, standing there, he made a bargain with God. He would walk through the town, and if he met Abe Trussler he would offer him the physick, if, that is, Abe was prepared to acknowledge him. If however he did not meet Abe, as it were accidentally, he would conclude that God did not intend him to make the offer. With that resolved he set out, briskly yet not so briskly that he could not nod to people as he passed, and keep eyes open for Abe.

He saw him when he was still a fair distance away. He was beside the road as if he was on his way somewhere but had stopped to lean against a roadside tree. What had stopped him was spasm after spasm of coughing.

He looked up as Hal drew near. He could not speak for coughing, and seemed about to shake his fist. Hal stood still beside him.

'Master Trussler, Sir,' he said. 'I've brought you some physick for your cough. It's made from horehound and that helps clear coughs.'

'Physick?' Abe croaked. 'Damned apothecaries.'

'Not an apothecary,' Hal said. 'Mistress Mannory made it. You know she understands about herbs and plants.'

'Mannory! Mannory!' Abe muttered. 'You one o' them.'

'I'm no one,' Hal ventured to say. 'Just an orphan.'

'Orphan, eh?' Abe stood a little taller and took a breath. 'So what if I'm your father?'

Hal said nothing.

'I might well be. I had your mother plenty of times in lieu of rent.' He coughed again. 'What's Tanner Mannory doing handing out physick? Out to poison me?'

'Nothing to do with Master Mannory. I just asked Mistress Mannory if she had something for coughs.'

Abe held out his hand.

'Just a spoonful and not too often, Mistress told me.' Hal handed over the bottle.

He did not wait after that. Suddenly he was overwhelmed by childhood memories long buried, of his mother and the men who came to her, of constant hunger, of Abe's apparent hatred of him. And suppose Abe was indeed his father? How did one learn to forgive all of that? Was it even reasonable to forgive it at all?

Chapter 9 - Ann's Cooking

A goodly smell greeted James as he opened the cottage door, a smell of stewing bacon. Yesterday had been market day, and Ann must have dawdled among the stalls, spending the money he had given her, or maybe she had attended the weekly lecture after the market closed at noon, and stayed to chat afterwards. Whatever the reason, the fire had not been lit when he came home for the midday meal, and all they had to eat was bread and cheese, not for the first time either. He kept hoping that when the shortening September days meant reverting to a full meal in the evening, Ann might manage better.

But today the smell was good and tempting, and Ann smiling. They sat down at the little table in front of the fire where she had laid out plates and bowls and cutlery and a loaf already sliced. She fished a chunky piece of bacon out of the cauldron and put it on a board for James to carve up, and then ladled broth and vegetables into the bowls.

The piece of bacon was long and fairly narrow. James started at one end and cut it into small slices which he laid on pieces of bread. He took a bite of bread and bacon, and then a spoonful of the broth in which leeks had shredded among the few carrots.

He looked across at Ann. She was fishing the bits of vegetable out of the broth and only nibbling at the bacon.

'I can't eat this!' he exclaimed.

'It is rather salty,' Ann said.

'Rather salty! Didn't you soak the bacon?'

'Soak it?' Ann said.

'Don't you know you have to soak bacon?' James said, 'Overnight in plenty of water.'

'I put it in plenty of water,' Ann said.

'And cooked it in the same water? Didn't you know you have to immerse it in water for hours, and throw the water away, and scrape off the bloom? Even I know that. I've seen my mother preparing bacon time out of number.'

Ann looked at him dumbly.

James stood up. 'I'm going back to the Tanyard. See what's left from their meal that I can eat. A month we've been married, and not one decent meal have you cooked.' He stormed out.

Back at Tanyard House his mother Phoebe, well used to weathering bouts of anger in husband or son, responded without reproach with a plate of delicious stew and home baked bread. She brought him a tankard of ale and sat silently on the bench opposite him until he had finished.

'Ann can't cook,' he muttered.

'Suppose,' Phoebe said tentatively, 'Suppose you both eat here for a while, and Ann comes and helps me prepare the food.'

James contemplated his calm, comfortable mother.

'She certainly won't ask help from her own mother, that's for sure. Do you think she'd learn from you?'

'You can ask her.'

'Ask? I'll tell her. That is what she has to do.'

Ann was hungry. She ate her slice of bread and bacon, and it was tasty if a little tough.

If James could storm out, so could she. She grasped the cauldron handle out of the fireplace. The handle was hot. She stuffed her singed fingers into her mouth, dived under the staircase to dip them in the bucket of cold water beside the sink. With growing indignation she grabbed a cloth to wrap around the cauldron handle. Then she carried it out through the back door, out and across the wagon yard as fast as she could go, to the river where she flung the contents, leeks, carrots and offending salty broth, into the water. She even knelt down and swilled out the pan, so that nothing at all was left of her scorned meal.

Back in the cottage, the sliced bacon lay on its board in a hardening puddle of fat. So much for James and his marvellous mother. She plumped herself down on her stool, and ate a slice. And then another, and another. After a while she became very thirsty. She went into the back room and dipped water out of the bucket, and drank and drank.

She could not endure staying indoors with the litter of discarded bowls and implements. She let herself out into the lane where she stood hesitating for a moment or two before heading uphill and past her family home.

It was Charity she wanted to see, to listen to her indignation, to hear how hard it was to be married to James. But it was Abigail who answered her knock, Abigail who welcomed her indoors amid the piles of leather and harnesses.

'Why, whatever is the matter?' she asked.

'Isn't Charity here?' Ann demanded.

'She's taken Simon out for a little walk,' Abigail said. 'What is troubling you, Ann?'

'Your brother!' Ann burst out. 'After all my work preparing bacon stew he refused to eat it and just stormed back to the tannery and your precious mother.'

Abigail smiled ruefully. 'Our mother is a very good cook,' she said. 'Didn't your mother teach you cooking?'

'There was always a cook. And mother used me for sewing with the girls.'

'I'm sorry.' Abigail laid her hand on Ann's shoulder. 'It is important to learn, especially now when food is so short.' She looked away. 'James' temper is short too at times. But he does love you.'

'He promised to love me, in that marriage service. It doesn't show though. How is it meant to show?'

'You've had only weeks so far to get used to living together,' Abigail said.

'I don't even like James some of the time,' Ann whispered. This good match she had made, this escape from her family, seemed to be having so many drawbacks. Her eyes filled with tears. Abigail put an arm round her and held her while she sobbed.

After a while Ralph came in from some errand. Ann wiped her eyes and Abigail picked up her needle.

Ann had washed the dishes with the water still warm on the dying fire, and had tidied both the cottage and herself by the time James returned at the end of work. His mother had mellowed his mood with the hope of improvements, but he remained firm.

'We are going to take our meals in the Tanyard,' he said, 'and you are going to help my mother and learn to cook.'

'Your… mother?' Ann stammered.

'You promised to love, honour and obey me, remember? So you will obey in this matter.'

Ann did not go to the Tanyard at first light as James did. Reluctantly, spurred by his stern injunction, she wandered over later. For once, the yard held no unpleasant smells. Even the dogs tethered at the gate seemed less defensive.

Phoebe saw her through the window and came out to greet her. There was no fire on the hearth. Ann followed her round the chimney stack into the bake room behind.

'The bread is just proving,' she said. 'Had you come earlier you could have kneaded it with me.'

'I buy bread from the baker in Church Lane,' Ann said.

'We feed so many mouths here,' Phoebe said. 'We'll fetch some vegetables. As the bread oven will be hot, we'll roast some parsnips.'

They went out into the vegetable plot at the back of the house. Phoebe handed Ann a fork. 'They root so firmly it takes a fork to dig them up,' she said.

Dig? Ann had never in her life, dug. Seeing her blank look, Phoebe took back the fork. 'You put it in a short distance from the parsnip so as not to damage the root with the fork tines.' She loosened the earth. 'Now you pull the root out.'

Some leaves broke off as Ann pulled, and she realised she would have to grasp the top of the root itself, all messy with damp earth. And then the earth had to be washed off, and the parsnips scraped, and herbs gathered and chopped, and some apples peeled and cut up, and so the morning wore on.

Phoebe formed the dough into loaves. She stuffed faggots of gorse into the oven with a handful of dry leaves, which she lit from the tinder box. The gorse, with more faggots added, flared with intense heat. She put the loaves in the embers with parsnips between, and closed the oven door. Sweat ran down her flushed face.

I don't want to look like that, Ann thought, and with an apron spattered with mud and vegetable juice. But when the meal came, with journeymen and apprentices, and James, Thomas and Hal gathered at the long table with Jacob and Phoebe and the servant girl, it was good.

She went home afterwards, and sat by the window sewing. James came in at dusk with a pleased look on his face and even kissed her. 'But,' she said, 'I can't see any purpose in my learning to make bread, for we do not have a bread oven, and a loaf from the baker feeds the two of us. And there are no vegetables in the garden to dig, or herbs. Today I might as well have been a servant.'

She did not go every day, though she never missed a meal. As September wore on and the days shortened, the main meal moved to the evening. Best then was the walk home with James in the twilight. Sometimes he held her hand, and she hoped this might lead to some tenderness when they were abed. But still he thrust into her in business-like fashion as her body tensed, and she began to turn away, to plead weariness, to resist him.

Sunday in early October they gathered in the Tanyard for a last midday meal.

'Ann dear,' Phoebe had said, 'I think I have taught you all you need to know to feed James and yourself. Just remember to think ahead, for fuel as well as food.'

For a moment Ann looked scared. All very well cooking what Phoebe had purchased or dug from the garden.

Phoebe caught her expression. 'Let's make a list to remind you for market day,' she said. She wrote down 'Faggots', then

Carrots, onions, turnips, butter, eggs, cheese, bacon... 'You can buy these to last all week.'

Ann mouthed the words as Phoebe wrote. If only she had paid as much attention to reading as she had done to sewing.

Thomas handed James a bundle of publications he had bought in London on his behalf from the St Paul's book women. James paid him and hurried Ann towards home, eager to start reading while the light lasted.

He placed a chair close to the window. Putting the news-books and pamphlets in date order on his knee, he began to read silently. Ann sat with her hands folded, gazing at the hearth, empty for several weeks in the warm autumn weather with no cooking to do. Faggots, bundles of small wood bound with twine, were stacked to one side where by now they must be well dried. She could forget them from the list for the time being.

James looked up. 'This makes absorbing reading,' he said. 'First there's *Heads of Proposals* put together by the Army. It seems General Ireton, Cromwell's son-in-law, had a lot to do with that. They took it to the King and he said he preferred the *Newcastle Propositions* which he'd rejected before, and then he rejected them again. There's no satisfying him.

'Here's an interesting new pamphlet, only 16 pages long and very clear, *What the Independents would have.* By a lawyer, John Cooke – if only all lawyers wrote this clearly. It includes everything the Levellers and all right minded people are campaigning for.'

Ann stood up and went into the back room, where she stayed for a while looking out of the window. When she came back James said, 'Listen to this. Cooke writes as if he's Jesus addressing the Army. "Your work is not yet done. You must stand up for the liberties of your brethren. Why have I empowered you, but to purchase liberty for my people?"' He looked up at her. 'Our hope surely is with the Army. The agitators, they were elected by the ordinary troopers, that's how it should be. They have been empowered by their fellows.'

Ann sat silently as if waiting for more. Then she said, 'James, if you could get some hurdles we could fence in the corner by the privy and have some hens.'

James looked up as if from a great distance. 'Hens....? What have hens to do with...? Ann, I've been reading matters of national importance. Do they not interest you at all?'

'Oh, I suppose freedom is a good idea, and you spend hours reading about it. But what use is reading? I can't see what you can actually do about it.'

James lowered the pamphlet onto his knee. 'We fought for liberty and justice,' he said, 'And now...' His tone quietened as his own words spoke to him. 'And now, what can one do, stuck out here. It's in the Army and in London that the action is.' Rather than the anger which his frustrations usually triggered, his remoteness from those working for reform was making him momentarily sad.

'What about hens, then?' Ann said.

He smiled a little wistfully at her. 'So, what about hens?' and he went out of the back door to inspect the possibilities.

Chapter 10 - Thomas

A question about harness took Thomas to the Attfields' house with a question. Hal had mended it repeatedly, and now Thomas thought some adaptation would be useful.

'Well!' Abigail exclaimed. 'Fancy seeing you! Where have you been all this time?'

'A lot to do,' Thomas muttered, 'and two days each week to and fro to London.'

'Come, you can sit down and eat with us and answer some of our questions.'

They sat around the table in the back room. Embers glowed in the fireplace and a single rush light illuminated the table. Abigail served the food, little Simon sitting sleepily on Charity's knee. Taken by surprise, Charity hardly looked at Thomas.

Conversation flowed around them. Ralph reported a gradual increase in demand for their harnesses. His failure to arrange an apprenticeship for Hal continued to frustrate him. Thomas in his turn was enthusiastic over his contract which had brought carting opportunities for the return journeys. He looked over at Charity from time to time but she did not look up.

'We hear some items of news,' Ralph said. 'James occasionally lends us one of the newsbooks he receives.'

Thomas laughed. 'His newsbooks and pamphlets are becoming part of my return load. He gets me to purchase them from St Paul's churchyard where women have stalls. Lord knows when he finds time to read them.'

'Presbyterianism, what do you think of it?' Ralph said. 'Is it any better than the old system with Bishops and such?'

'It's meant to be more democratic,' Thomas said, 'but it's still about control.'

'When we were in Cropredy,' Abigail said, 'believers used to congregate in Mother Metcalfe's cottage and we had some blessed times. Someone would read from the Bible, sometimes we sang, always we prayed for one another and for whatever arose that needed prayer.'

'There was a freedom,' Ralph said. 'No one lorded it over the others, and we moved as the Holy Spirit seemed to be prompting.'

'Not that we were all the same,' Abigail said. 'One or two men had a real gift for expounding scripture and one woman in particular was often called upon to pray for healing or release. Is there anything like that in Farnham?'

'Father says the new Minister, as he likes to be called, is Presbyterian. There's some organisation being set up to supervise everything from Godalming,' Thomas said.

Abigail turned to Charity. 'What was your experience, at home?'

Charity looked up, confused. 'I... we... went to church at Easter. It was a long walk.' She stood up, with Simon now fast asleep in her arms. 'I'll put Simon to bed,' she said, and went up the stairs.

Abigail turned to Thomas. 'She is a sweet girl, so helpful, but Tom we still know nothing about her, why you brought her here. Isn't it time you told us?'

Thomas pushed his plate aside and leant his elbows on the table, his head in his hands. Then, aware of Ralph, Abigail and Hal silently waiting, he said 'I was travelling from Bath.'

'Battle of Lansdowne!' Ralph exclaimed. 'You brought Hal to be my paddy boy!'

Thomas nodded. 'We'd gone down with a heavy load. Pay for the troops I think it was. And they got me moving gunpowder.'

Ralph turned to Abigail. 'All General Waller's Army was quartered in and around Bath,' he said. 'Several skirmishes we had before the actual battle began.'

They could have continued talking about those days, about Thomas trailing the soldiers as they were moved from one strategic hill to another, and then the noise and action and confusion and smoke of the battle. But Abigail said 'From Bath?'

'Yes,' Thomas said. 'I didn't rightly know where I was heading. I just wanted to leave Bath. It was filthy and running out of food. I found myself in Chippenham. Held by Royalists. They'd had victory in another battle. They took me on to carry a load of their loot to Oxford. That was the Royalist headquarters.'

'Just you and the cart?' Abigail said.

'Well, no.' Thomas shook his head. 'An escort of troopers on their horses. They commandeered a farm on the way for the night. I slept in my cart.'

He paused, searching for words, reluctant to elaborate. All he could bring himself to say was, 'Charity was in the farm house.'

He stood up, and went out into the darkness.

Strange how vividly that journey from Bath to Oxford had been called to mind by their questions. Even the chaos and bloodshed of the Lansdowne battle paled into comparison, in his memory, with the events at the farm. Faced in Bath with filth, food shortages and no prospect of a load to pay for his return home, he had set off in the first likely direction he came across, over the bridge and roughly north-east. He made a few miles that day, stopping at a farm where folk were willing to receive him and had provision.

'You from Bath?' the goodwife said. 'General Waller? Sounds as if you're on the winning side. We needs to keep in with yous.'

'I'm not really part of the Army,' Thomas said.

Continuing along the road the next day he was overtaken by Parliamentary cavalry. No one seemed interested in his empty cart, though some of the infantry following on laughingly called for a lift. They were all in high spirits.

Ahead lay Chippenham. Troops were everywhere. Seeing skirmishes in the fields either side of the road Thomas concluded that many of those he could see must be Royalist. He decided to go into the town. With evening Royalist troops were pouring inside, such a press that he could scarcely move the cart. The gates were closed behind the last of them, behind him. Thomas was at a loss to know where to park, where to sleep.

As he was wondering an officer came by and peered at the cart.

'My good man,' he said, 'you ought to know that the baggage train is set up the other side of the town.'

'I'm not part of the baggage train, Sir,' Thomas said.

'Are you for King or Parliament?'

'Not either, Sir. I'm just wanting to get home to Surrey.'

'Surrey! So you're not averse to long distances.'

'No Sir,' Thomas said, 'And I'd be glad of a load.'

'Ah.' The officer looked him up and down. 'You may be just what we're seeking. Come with me.'

He led Thomas into the servants' quarters of what was clearly one of the best houses in the town. Cooks were attempting to conjure up a meal amid a throng of armed men filling the passageways. Thomas made himself as inconspicuous as he could until the officer returned.

'Right my man,' he said. 'My Lord Hertford has a deal of loot which needs to be carried to safety. You will load it onto your cart in the morning and take it to Oxford. You will be provided with an escort.'

Hardly able to believe his luck, Thomas managed to thank him, and then boldly added 'Would you be pleased to pay me something in advance?'

The officer again looked him up and down, and finally said 'I will enquire of the Marquess.'

Secure overnight in the stable yard, it was not until the chests and bundles were loaded into the cart in the morning and he emerged with the escort of a dozen horsemen, some coins newly in his pocket, that Thomas realised the degree of activity going on. Weary troops were re-grouping to go and face Waller's Army outside the town, and he was glad to be departing in the opposite direction.

For much of the day they rode in silence. Maybe the escorting troopers were glad to be temporarily away from the fighting, though they never relaxed their watch on the surrounding countryside, wary of ambush. The sunshine was thundery hot.

Towards the end of the afternoon the Lieutenant in charge of the escort drew up beside a sizeable farm fronting the road.

'As good a quarter as we'll find,' he said, and wheeled into the farmyard shouting 'Ho! Farmer!'

An old man with a long white beard came out of a barn holding a pitchfork. He was holding it as one would hold a tool at rest, vertical, but seeing the Lieutenant and the troopers behind him, he slowly lowered it to the angle of a pike.

'We'll quarter here tonight old man,' the Lieutenant said.

The farmer brandished his pitchfork. The Lieutenant laughed. 'Lay it down old man. We're more than a match for you.'

His eyes fearful, the farmer lunged towards the Lieutenant's horse. He, quick as a flash, drew his sword and swiped the pitchfork from his hands.

'Enough of that. Don't force me to kill you.'

Slowly the farmer found his voice. 'I'll not have soldiers quartered on my farm.'

'You'll do as I say.' The Lieutenant gestured to the party outside to move into the yard. With troopers all around him, Thomas could not but move too.

'Twelve men and mounts and the carter with his two horses, and somewhere secure for the cart. That barn looks convenient.' He rode towards the high doorway through which loaded carts would be driven in. 'Ah, sweet smelling hay! Good for man and beast.'

'You'll not sleep in there!' the farmer wailed. ''T'is new hay newly mown and newly stacked.'

The Lieutenant looked at him and then speculatively at the house. 'Very well, we'll quarter in the house. Tell them to prepare beds and a good supper.'

At this point the door opened revealing the farmer's wife,

almost as old but big and stout with grey hair strained back under a kerchief. With one glance she took in the scene in the yard, the cart, the horses milling about, the men, the Lieutenant still holding his sword, and her husband cowering by the barn door, his pitchfork on the ground at his feet.

'Whose men are these?' she asked loudly.

'The King's troopers,' the Lieutenant said, 'requiring lodging and food.'

'I've no food to give you.'

As if on cue a squawk of chickens skittered across the end of the yard pursued by a large cockerel.

'You've food a-plenty,' the Lieutenant said. 'Kill the cockerel.'

'Oh no!' Her hands flew over her mouth, but two men had already drawn their pistols and spurred their horses behind the farm buildings. Two shots rang out, and their laughter.

'Not the cockerel,' they said, returning. 'A succulent goose.'

They laughed again and were congratulated. The farmer's wife wrung her hands.

'Now Gamma, prepare it for our supper,' the Lieutenant said. 'Gaffer, show me stabling for the horses. And Gamma, we need beds for a dozen men.'

Surely, Thomas thought, this aged couple were not alone on this big farm. He followed round to the barn which must shelter cows in the winter, where he unhitched the cart and tended his horses. 'I'll sleep here with the cart,' he said.

'You'll need a guard,' the Lieutenant said. 'I'll set two a couple of hours turn about. If you're attacked we'll hear from the house quickly enough.'

For a moment when Thomas was by the barn door he

thought he caught sight of a girl, a young woman, running off across the fields. There must be farm workers, sons, even grandsons. Perhaps they were all out in the fields harvesting. Was she summoning them home? He imagined them coming in force, armed with reaping hooks and pitchforks, lethal weapons against both men and horses. Or perhaps she was warning the men not to come home, arranging for them to spend the night in the open rather than risk confrontation.

Once the horses were settled the men, led by the Lieutenant, walked into the house. Thomas stayed behind, where the old man was still hovering.

'I'm sorry,' he said. 'They know you can't stand up against them.'

'If my sons were here...' the old man quavered.

'There could be a bloody battle,' Thomas said. 'It could cost you dear.'

The old man grunted and went to retrieve his pitchfork. Indoors, Thomas could hear argument. He went to see what was happening.

Hands on hips the old woman was repeating that she had no claret. 'We've not strong drink in this house nor ever will have, and this the Lord's day,' she said. She stood foursquare beside the fireplace where portions of goose were sizzling in a wide pan.

'We'll soon see,' the Lieutenant said. Several doors opened out of the kitchen. He pulled out some jars from one saying 'We'll have those.' The third door opened onto a staircase and they all heard a squeal and a footfall, and glimpsed the flash of a skirt. 'Ah,' he said, eyes gleaming. The last door was the one he sought, leading down to the cellar where they blundered about, finding only logs.

'So where's the ale Gamma?'

She gestured to yet another door which opened to reveal several barrels, and cheese lined up on shelves. With triumphant cries they hauled the cheese out and started hacking at them with their daggers.

'Not all of them!' the woman pleaded. 'You don't need to open up all them cheeses!'

'What we don't eat now we'll take with us. Tankards woman! We need to drink!'

And drink they did, spilling ale on the floor as they filled and re-filled and drank and drank. Thomas felt no desire to get drunk in their company. Then the woman sliced loaves of bread and served goose, and they gorged themselves. Hungry as he had been, Thomas saw no point in eating more than satisfied him. The goose was tasty if tough, and when he had had enough he quietly withdrew to the barn and his cart. The guards ran in to secure their share.

After a while another pair wandered over, and Thomas wondered how long they would stay awake and what use they would be as guards. He piled one or two bundles in the cart and curled up in the resulting space for a fitful sleep. Noise and loud voices from the house disturbed it, footsteps across the yard and a door closing, and once he thought he heard a scream.

He woke stiff and frowsty. As he had anticipated, the two guards were sound asleep propped against the doorposts. Of the rest there was no sign. He uncurled himself and stretched, and Blaze and Star whinnied. His good friends.

Out in the yard he splashed his face in the horse trough and felt better. He found a bucket and filled it for the horses. He longed to hitch up the cart and go, but he did not know the way to Oxford nor could he leave without the escort.

A dog barked. A shed door slowly creaked open and the old man peeped out. Seeing only Thomas he emerged. 'Where are they all?' he whispered.

'Ate and drank themselves stupid I reckon,' Thomas said almost as quietly.

'They are devils, wicked.' The old man's whisper was vehement. 'My good wife talks only of murdering them in their beds, and if she did we are all as good as dead.'

The door creaked again to allow the woman herself through it. She held a large knife.

'Sarah my dear... he whimpered.

'This is one of them,' she snarled, the knife held perilously towards Thomas.

'No my dear, no, this is just the carter. He has been in the cart all night.'

'I beg you madam, do not fight them,' Thomas said.

'I fought them indoors, but then I didn't have my knife. God! I would have castrated that Lieutenant.'

The old man laid a trembling hand on Thomas's arm. 'Our granddaughter was in there, our precious motherless child. I fear for her.'

'I thought I saw a woman run across the fields,' Thomas said.

'Our daughter. She ran to warn her betrothed and the men. At least she is saved...' and he began to weep. His wife growled. Thomas thought fast.

'We cannot undo what has been done, but I will try to get them all away quickly. Do you hide in the shed where you were. It is the only way.'

'But the child,' the woman wailed.

'I will see she suffers no harm,' Thomas said with much more confidence than he felt.

He saw the old pair into the shed with their dog, and bracing himself, went into the house. He listened. He heard someone moving about upstairs - at least one of them was awake. Through the door and up the stairs where he had glimpsed that flash of a skirt. Again he stood listening, trying to locate the movement he had heard.

Suddenly a girl's voice cried, 'No! No! Leave me be! Get away!' instantly muffled.

He knocked thunderously at the door, and again, and again. He went on knocking until the Lieutenant, bleary eyed, stopped shouting abuse and opened it. He stank of beer and sweat.

'What in hell do you want?'

'We must start away. There are troops on all the roads, King or Parliament I know not... Thomas was talking fast, anything that came into his head. 'The Marquess's baggage must reach Oxford. The old man's peasants will be bringing in the hay armed with pitchforks, double pronged pikes. They'll kill your horses. Lord Hertford...'

'Damn you!' the Lieutenant said, and past him Thomas could see a girl watching desperately from the bed. He went on pressing the need to move off.

'Stop gabbling man,' the Lieutenant said. 'Go and wake the blackguards and put the cheeses in the cart and anything else you can purloin. We'll not go empty handed.'

Thomas stood his ground, aware of the girl in the bed.

The Lieutenant fumbled with his breeches, slid his feet

into his long boots, heaved on his buff coat and reached for his sword. He was buckling on the sword belt when he too caught sight of the girl. Drawing the sword out of its scabbard he said, 'I might as well finish off this slut.'

Thomas leapt to grab both his wrists. He reeled back. The sword clattered onto the floor.

'Lay off!'

'I'll kill you myself if you touch her!'

'Oh valiant knight!' The Lieutenant recovered his balance. 'You're only a common carter! Do you want her for yourself?'

'I want to rescue what remains of her honour.'

'Honour! What do you know about honour, carter!' He struggled to free himself. In a swift movement Thomas put both hands on his right wrist and twisted his arm behind his back, a wrestling trick long learnt.

'How dare you fight an officer!'

'How dare you threaten a woman!'

'I'll have you hung for this.'

'And the Marquess's belongings?' Still gripping the twisted arm with one hand Thomas bent and picked up the sword. 'If I take your sword do I not take your honour?'

Their noise had finally woken the men who began to emerge from the bedrooms to see what was happening. At once Thomas released the Lieutenant. His authority over the escort was necessary. They must not see his humiliation.

'Your sword, Sir,' he said, handing it to him as if nothing had happened.

The Lieutenant almost spat at him as he strode out of the room, issuing orders left and right.

The sooner they left, the better for the family. Thomas

could hear gunfire not far off, and someone muttered that they must be attacking Devizes. At last, leaving the barn littered with hay and manure, they set out towards Oxford, a silent surly group.

And that was all. He did not know the girl's name, nor anything about her, except her plight. Yet all these years the memory had persisted, the sense that he should return to the farm, he knew not why nor for what purpose. It was too much to try to explain to Ralph and Abigail, too close to risk the emotions it might arouse.

Chapter 11 - Monarchy

William Kiffin had a Bible and paper spread over the table. He was struggling, unusually for him, to formulate a sermon when Hanna returned from shopping. Having deposited her purchases in the kitchen, she came and put her arm round William's shoulders and kissed his cheek. 'Have you inspiration?' she said.

'No.' He closed the lid of his inkwell and sitting back, looked up smiling. 'You look as if you have something to tell me.'

'I met Mary Overton,' she said. 'Richard is released from prison. They are back in their home, and their children with them.'

'Good news indeed,' William said. 'Do they need help?'

'Thomas Lambe was there – I went with Mary to the house – and some of their congregation. I bought a few necessities for them.'

Her fingers strayed to the open Bible, flicking through the pages until she found the first book of Samuel. 'Richard and Lambe were talking about how, when Samuel was Judge over Israel, he warned the Israelites that having a king was not a good idea. Look, I've found it, in the first book of Samuel. "He'll make soldiers of your sons" – King Charles did that,'

'And so did Parliament,' William said.

'"Some will serve in war chariots, or cavalry, or be officers in charge of men".'

'It sounds like the New Model Army.'

'And then it goes on that he'll take the best land and

vineyards, and the people will have to work his land, and be cooks and perfumers. And he'll levy taxes, a tenth of everything. Isn't that very high taxation?'

'High taxes without consent were a reason for the war.' William ran his finger up the column of print. 'See the start of the chapter. It looks as if Samuel was trying to create a dynasty in his old age, appointing his own sons to be judges like him. And they were dishonest, taking bribes and so on. A so-called theocracy, or a republic, doesn't guarantee good government.'

'But Samuel wasn't elected, was he,' Hanna said. 'Richard said that in a republic, citizens vote for their ruler.' She looked at William as another thought struck her. 'Just as you were elected to be Pastor by the Baptist congregation.'

William nodded thoughtfully. 'One has to hope that that was under God's guidance.'

'A theocracy?' Hanna said.

'Well, no,' William said. 'An attempt to run the church on New Testament lines. Parliament is different, however godly some members are. There seems to be much self-interest, and fear of opposition. Power seems to do that to people.'

'So you'd not be in favour of a republic?'

'I don't know. It depends on who votes, who gets into the seat of power.'

'Who makes the rules,' Hanna added. 'Like you do, Will, for our congregation. Such as the rule that only those who have been baptised by immersion may be members.'

'It was the decision of the congregation as a body,' William said. He drew the Bible towards him, turning the pages back to where he had been reading.

Hanna was not to be deterred. 'So what about the King?' she said.

'According to the agent Philip,' William said, 'several groups are negotiating with the King. Philip suspects he plays off one against the other, Presbyterians versus Independents and so on. With all the struggling for power, it's tempting to think we'd be better off with the King reinstated. But that has to be on new terms, so that his power is constrained.'

'Constrained by whom?'

'Hanna, you are becoming quite the debater,' he laughed. 'Parliament I suppose. When I last saw John Lilburne, still in the Tower, he was veering towards restoring the King. Preferable, he said, to having Cromwell in control.'

He closed the Bible. 'What about my going to see the King and finding out his position for myself?'

'You?' Hanna said.

'Yes, me. Why not? Not as Baptist Pastor – he suspects Baptists - but as a wealthy merchant. He might be glad to see anyone with something to suggest. Now that he's in custody in Hampton Court I could go up on the flood tide, gain an audience and return on the ebb. I must check when tides will next be right.'

He stood up, and Hanna hugged him. 'Action!' she said. 'Dear Will.'

Hampton Court was well guarded. Having gained entry William was led, not to the throne room but to a drawing room. He recognised one or two of the gentlemen sitting with King Charles, who received him graciously.

He was charming, this small man. 'You dealt with the

guard,' he said. 'I have given my word that I will not attempt to escape my palace which they have made into a prison, but they insist on a guard,' he said.

He seemed to be well informed of all that was happening, and gave such assurances of liberty for the future that when William bowed himself from the room he felt satisfied of his goodwill. Even Hanna's scepticism did not deflect him from letting John Lilburne know his conclusions.

Betty Gary sat on a high stool beside the parlour window. It gave her the light she needed for sewing, (and supervising Eliza and Jane now that Ann was gone) while being ideally placed to observe goings-on in the streets outside.

From her perch she caught sight of Charity walking down the hill, holding little Simon by one hand and a basket in the other. It was not the first time she had seen her go by. Where did she go? If it were just to the baker, she seemed to take a long time on the errand. Or did she call on Ann, who seemed to be friendly with her? Hadn't she ridden to Farnham with Thomas Mannory? Ah! Perhaps these walks were to see him. Tantalised by the very little she knew about Charity apart from her skill with the needle, she remained watching longer than her sewing justified.

Charity's destination was the wide meadow beyond the wagon yard, a green water meadow separated from the Tanyard by the river Wey. Simon was becoming sturdy and energetic. Her walks with him extended week by week. Abigail, grateful for an hour to work without distraction, thanked her regularly. Charity had no need of thanks, she delighted in their explorations. The meadows once discovered had become Simon's favourite place. "Walk!" he would demand, almost dragging her out.

Harvest was in the hedges, crab apples and rowan berries, and sloes too. Simon put one of the apples in his mouth, but one bite taught him their bitterness. He spat it out. 'They have to be cooked,' Charity said. 'See how many you can put into the basket.' She managed to reach down a few sprays of rowan too, hoping she could remember how her grandmother used to make a relish. Simon ran about, always within her sight.

'Home now,' she said at last, her basket full, 'and we'll get some bread on the way.'

It was as she came round the corner from Church Lane that Betty spotted her, standing right opposite the house window, and she and Simon were not alone. That silent lad Hal was beside her, the one who folk said talked to horses more than to people. Yet they were in animated conversation. Then he picked Simon up and lifted him onto his shoulders. Charity tried to steady the child, but he waved his arms in the air with a delighted giggle, and they laughed back at him before proceeding up the last incline and out of sight.

Well! Here was an interesting titbit. Everyone knew that Hal was a kind of orphan, even if, as was said, Jacob Mannory had fathered him. Rumour had it that Charity really was an orphan, though no one seemed to know why she was living with Abigail and her wounded husband. Judging by their animated chatting together, it looked as if Hal and Charity were familiar with one another. Who knew to what that might lead. More bastards? Maybe orphans were drawn to fellow orphans, though Lord knows they'd not have much future together.

Michael Gary when he came home was an unresponsive

recipient of her latest piece of gossip. 'Hal was probably going to eat with the Attfields,' he said. 'Hal was Ralph's horse boy in the Army for years you know.'

Betty had no option but to store up her piece of information and its putative implications until she met with her favoured gossip, Joan's mother, on Sunday.

Charity had been almost towing Simon up the cobbles of Church Lane. He was tired, and objecting to further walking when Hal caught up with them. She was grateful for Hal's help, and Simon loved him. His company was undemanding, like she imagined a brother might be.

Hal did not mean to take advantage of Thomas' absence to see Abe Trussler, one bright sunny October day. But as he passed Abe's yard in the normal course of business, one of Abe's men was chatting to a friend at the entrance. He recognised Hal from the wheel episode and hailed him cheerily. Hal jumped down from the cart.

'How is Mr. Trussler?' he asked.

'He's gloom and doom, for all this is a beautiful day,' the man replied. 'Hasn't hardly been out of his house.'

'Trusts you to carry on,' his companion said.

'Trusts? He'll come out of a sudden, and let fly. Always finds something wrong.'

'I wonder you stop with him,' the other man said.

'It's my trade,' he replied. 'And you can't help pity the man. No family, and even the women employed to keep house for him don't stay.'

'How's his cough?' Hal said.

'Someone gave him a bottle of physick, but he still coughs.'

Hal considered, and came to a decision. 'Mind my horse for a moment would you? I'll pop in and see him.'

'Rum chap,' the men agreed as Hal went towards the house. 'Who'd choose to beard Abe in his den?'

And den it was. Bed, chairs, table, cooking pots were all in the one room and everything was filthy. Abe was half in half out of the bed. He looked up as Hal, receiving no response to his knock, let himself in.

'Oh, it's you,' Abe croaked. 'That physick ain't no good.'

Faced with such chaos and neglect, Hal felt at a loss. All he could think of to say was 'Is there anything I can do for you?'

Abe looked him up and down, uncomprehending. A long silence between them. Then he said, 'You can fetch Niblett the attorney.'

The men were still by his cart when he returned to it, a question on both their faces. 'He wants me to fetch the attorney,' Hal said.

'It'll be some law suit or other,' the tanner said.

Chapter 12 - Temper

James walked round the yard, checking men and boys all occupied in one or other of the many tasks. Even the apprentice he had beaten so mercilessly in the Spring seemed to be making progress. The lad might never excel at all the aspects of tanning, but perhaps he might do as a beamsman. He was taking care with the hide draped over the convex beam, scudding it clear of impurities. Nathan Armstrong, head beamsman, stood by as instructor.

James addressed Nathan. 'It's tomorrow I'm going to London.'

Nathan nodded. 'I'd not forgotten,' he said. 'I'll make sure everything runs smoothly while you're away.'

James called to another apprentice to push the hand cart, and together they made their way across the bridge and up Snow Hill to Wilkins' workshop. It was already afternoon. The currier looked up from the big mahogany table where he was working oils into a heavy hide. He wore no shirt, the exertion of his strong compact muscles warming him even on this late October day.

'The skins?' James asked

'Is it today you're wanting them?' Wilkins barely paused in his kneading and pummelling.

'I told you I needed them today,' James said.

'The days slip by.' Wilkins shifted the angle of the hide under his hands.

'That's no way to do business. Are the skins ready?'

'Oh aye.' Wilkins straightened his back. 'But they're not sorted and bagged. When do you want them?'

'I wanted them now.' James was emphatic. 'I'll leave the handcart here for you to load and come back later.' The day was so short at this time of year.

He sent the apprentice back to the Tanyard, going part way with him until he reached the stable and granary that Thomas rented.

Thomas and Hal were heaving sacks into the big cart. 'Hullo!' Thomas said. 'I was wondering where you were. How many bundles do you need to stow?'

'That dullard Wilkins doesn't have them ready. I don't know how many. And can you keep them dry?'

'Of course we keep the load dry,' Thomas exclaimed. 'I'd not be thanked for delivering damp flour, now would I.'

James walked up and down, round the cart, in their way, until abruptly he left. Back to the Tanyard.

Jacob met him. 'Where's the handcart?' he demanded.

'I've left it at Wilkins to load with skins.'

'Skins? What's he doing with skins?'

'I told you. Thomas and I are taking them to London tomorrow.'

'Both of you?'

'Yes. I'm staying the week. Making contact with traders and so on.'

'Skins! You don't need the handcart for a few skins.'

'There are a lot. Several tanners have brought them in for currying and for me to sell on.'

'Trading! Taking you out of the tannery where your job is. And November too. Not enough hours in the day, and you

148

walk out. Do you expect me to act as my own foreman?'

'I've arranged for Nathan Armstrong to take my place for the week.'

'You've arranged! I make the appointments here.'

'It's hardly an appointment!' James almost shouted. 'A substitute for a week! Can't you trust me?'

'I'm not sure I can.' Jacob was equally vehement. 'Infiltrating all this fine skin curing into my yard, spending time at the curriers, and now this jaunt to London…'

'Jaunt!' James interrupted. 'It's work! You've had some of the proceeds. The use of "your" yard is paid for. You never want to change. As it was with your father and grandfather so it has to be for ever and ever.'

'If you're so keen for change, you'd better set up on your own. You'd know then the reality of profit and loss.'

'Is that how little you value me? Is that your opinion of how I run the yard?'

He strode out into the lane. Across the bridge and up to the currier.

'Well,' as he entered the workshop, 'Ready?'

Wilkins gestured to hessian sacks lined up against the wall. 'Deer skins there, calf, goat, rabbit, each kind separate. Here's the list, and the invoice.'

'I need them on the cart,' was all James said.

'You taking them now? It's almost dark.'

With the sacks on the handcart James set out, refusing the offer of a lantern. It was indeed almost dark, but he could make out the road between the houses, and wove his way down to Thomas' stabling.

Thomas had a lantern lit. They settled the sacks among the

sacks of flour and grain, and then Thomas lashed a double layer of tarpaulin over the load.

'I'll sleep here tonight,' he said. 'You'd better too if we're to start out before first light. Bring a blanket.'

'I've the handcart to take back to the Tanyard before I go home.'

Now it really was dark. Thomas did not offer a lantern. James tussled with the cart, fighting it as it stuck and slewed. He kicked the dogs inside the Tanyard gate when they bounded out on their chains.

He stuck his head round the house door. Supper was long over, the table cleared except for the big Bible from which Jacob would have read aloud to the household. How good it might have been, James thought wryly, if he'd read what one of the epistles said: "Fathers, provoke not your children to wrath".'

Without going into the room James called out 'I've left the handcart by the gate.' Jacob looked up. 'It's pitch black out here,' James said, and left.

Back again, past the dogs, along the lane, over the bridge, past Thomas' stable and round along Church Lane to the cottage. He stomped in.

Ann was standing by a dead fire, a single taper burning. Fragments of bread and cheese littered the table.

'So this is my supper is it, your leftovers!' He picked up a dry end of bread and threw it at her.

'You're so late,' Ann said, 'I thought you must have eaten at Tanyard House.'

'You thought, did you. Well, I didn't, and now what is there to eat?'

He went to the cupboard beside the chimney breast, and

opened the door. 'Nothing! Nothing! You can't even keep house!'

He hit her across the face, twice. 'Haven't you learnt anything?' He hit her again, with his fist.

She put her hands to her burning cheek and dived out of his way. Dived for the staircase. Stumbled up the steps, tripping as she went. Stood trembling by the bedpost.

He was after her. He pulled up her skirt and threw her onto the bed. 'There's only one thing you're good for,' he said, and with breeches barely pulled down he thrust into her, his hand over her mouth as she screamed.

He did not wait after that. He pulled a blanket off the bed, grabbed the few things he would need next day, and left.

On the Sunday, James went with the Kiffins to Devonshire Street, to the Baptist congregation which William pastored. They welcomed him warmly, so that he did not feel strange, yet the worship was different from the formal forms of the now banned Book of Common Prayer or the newly prescribed Presbyterian prayer book. There was a freedom with even some contributions by members of the congregation. At the same time it was firmly led by Thomas Patient, William's colleague.

Patient preached at length, with frequent reference to the Bible, his theme being God's forgiveness and the need to forgive one another. James heard it as an intellectual exercise rather than having personal application, an exercise which, because of the way it was presented, nonetheless fixed it into his mind, his memory.

When the service concluded he watched while people spoke with William and with Hanna too. Gradually they dispersed and William turned to him.

'Would you care to visit John Lilburne with me?' he asked. 'Hanna will take our daughter home.'

James accepted eagerly and together they walked down to the Tower.

Lilburne was not alone. 'Colonel Rainsborough,' he said, 'Fresh from the Army's debating at Putney.' He gestured them to stools. 'I was called to make my own case for release from prison on Thursday, so I have had to leave debating to others. Rainsborough is kindly come to tell me what befell.'

'The General Council is remarkable in itself,' Rainsborough said. 'To have Agitators elected by the common soldiery sitting down with officers and Generals and encouraged to speak freely – that is remarkable.'

'And do they speak freely?'

'Sexby – isn't he one of your chief contacts with the Army, Lilburne? – fairly pitched into Commissary General Ireton and Lieutenant General Cromwell at the start. "You two," he said, and of course everyone knows Ireton is married to Cromwell's daughter. Cromwell dealt with him well, though he is not always at ease as chairman. I sense he is eager to move things along, and favours committees.'

'Two agents from each regiment?' Lilburne asked.

'Not at first, but word was sent back to the five regiments quartered in Putney that they should attend, and there are advisers as well, your friend Richard Overton among them. There is no agenda, anyone is free to speak.

'And do they?'

'Some speak, and to good effect. But the debate easily becomes muddied. Ireton seems to assemble his thoughts by speaking. This means that what he says is often unclear until perhaps at the very end he makes a definite statement.' He chuckled. 'At one point he and I were truly at loggerheads and Cromwell told us to calm down.

'What was the subject?' William asked

'There were two, which complicates things. That young lawyer Wildman, whom the soldiers asked to be their mouthpiece, had a hand in writing *The case of the Army truly stated*. Then they decided to simplify that and produced another paper *An Agreement of the People*. A committee was meant to have examined both of them, but Ireton claimed they were new to him.'

'Not a promising beginning,' Lilburne said.

'The discussion was soon bogged down about engagements, and to what extent you are bound by an agreement, an engagement, depending on whether such an engagement is just or unjust. And then on to the King's injustice, and that the power should be with the people.'

'You believe in a republic, don't you?' Lilburne said. 'I have doubts about that. A properly negotiated agreement restoring the King seems to me the better way.'

'Was anything resolved in your debating?' William asked.

'Early on the first day, Thursday, Lieutenant Colonel Goffe urged us to seek God's will before proceeding further. So after more words – and Cromwell did urge us to move on – it was agreed that Friday morning would be devoted to prayer, not compulsory but for everyone so moved, and that we reassemble in the afternoon. And so it went on.'

'Words, words,' James said.

'Ireton objected that the Army considered their paper *An Agreement* to be so clear, so infallible, that anyone wanting to dilute it or disagree with it was doing something unlawful. He has a liking for *The Heads of the Proposals* which he and General Fairfax produced months ago and offered to the King, who shilly-shallied and got them to dilute it. We were meant to be considering the *Agreement* clause by clause. More than once Cromwell pressed to defer the debate and nominate a committee.'

'Committees can be safer than full debate,' Lilburne said.

'Well, the day ended with a committee appointed, a good mixture of officers and agents with some civilians including Overton.'

'And what of Friday?' Lilburne asked.

'I was unwell that morning so I arrived after discussion had begun. Some good points were made – the dangers of delay, the danger of division. Then it moved on to who should be allowed to vote. I said that every man that is to live under a government ought first by his own consent put himself under that government. That got Ireton going. All to do with quali-fication by property, land ownership.'

'But that's how it is now,' James said. 'Based on land and corporations.'

'Yes, but excluding servants. The argument is that being dependent on the will of their master they would be afraid to displease him and so would not vote freely. A red herring was that foreigners resident in England should not be allowed a voice in our elections. For fear we'd be led into anarchy. Cromwell actually came to our defence then. Wildman supported me, saying that every person in England has as clear a right as the greatest person in England to elect his representative.'

'Haven't I always written, proclaimed, that right!' Lilburne exclaimed. 'Since the Norman conquest we have been enslaved. And what have we been fighting for, but our freedom?'

'And so it was forcibly said. Thousands have ventured their lives and their estates, such as they were, to recover our birthright as Englishmen. One of the agents quoted a Latin tag, "that which concerns all, ought to be debated by all."'

'So now you await the committee's conclusions, do you?'

'We re-assemble tomorrow,' Rainsborough said.

'Is the whole Army represented?' James asked.

'Five regiments,' Rainsborough said. 'Three are absent, still engaged against Royalist troops in different pockets.'

'Can civil war ever gain outright victory?' William Kiffin mused.

'That is why reforming Parliament towards a strong government is vital,' Lilburne said.

After a while William said 'Come James, we had best leave these gentlemen to prepare for the morrow.'

'Master Kiffin!' The shout halted them as they walked back up through the City.

'Master Kiffin!' A man was hurtling towards them. He stopped, breathless, beside them.

'Master Kiffin! I'm so glad to have seen you. I wanted to tell you. I've almost found her.'

William looked at him, this eager man in his thirties. 'Found?' he said.

'My daughter. I told you about her when I read to your Lydia. I can hardly contain myself for joy. She is alive, and well. I don't know where. Not yet. Oh! Master Kiffin! So marvellous to have got this far!'

'A daughter.' William was struggling to remember the conversation. 'You said the mother died. In the New World or the Old?'

'I left her behind because she was so near her time. I heard nothing until Master Woodbridge's father sent a note - remarkable that it reached me at all – to tell me that she had died but the girl child had survived. He had officiated at her funeral – he's Rector at Stanton Fitzwarren where we come from. Her mother might never have told me. There was no love lost between her and me.' He took breath. 'That woman hasn't changed, I can tell you, but at least she didn't throw me out. At the farm I mean. Master Woodbridge went to visit his father at Stanton Fitzwarren and I went with him, back to our old haunts, not far from the farm.'

'And did you meet the daughter?' William asked.

'Alas! No. She wasn't there. Her grandmother sent her away, Lord knows where. It seemed strange, and she would not tell me anything beyond that the girl had gone.'

William turned to James. 'This young man, (Walter Hutchcroft isn't it?) is employed by Preacher John Woodbridge from Massachusetts. Woodbridge is lately come over to England to be chaplain to those who are trying to negotiate with the King.'

'A frustrating role,' Walter said. 'Every time a new discussion with the King is set up he expects to be called upon, but none lasts long, so he remains in London. Our lodgings are all arranged now, so we felt free to make that visit.'

'Allow me to introduce you to my friend, James Mannory,' William said.

'Mannory, did you say? James Mannory?'

'That is my name,' James said.

'Mannory. Mannory. That name is connected in some way with this business.'

'Not with me, I assure you,' James said.

Charity never knew why she had knocked on Ann's door that particular morning. It was too early even for the bread to be baked in the bakery next door. Abigail had looked surprised to see her wrap a shawl around her shoulders and go out into the barely light street. She just said 'Going out?' and Charity had simply nodded.

The door was ajar, so when no one responded to her knock she cautiously pushed it open and went inside. Beyond the stairs a feeble light was burning in the back room.

'Ann?' she called. 'May I come in?'

A sort of moan came from the back room. When Charity went through Ann looked up from the sink where she was standing. 'Oh, it's you,' was all she said.

She had the sink full of water. Cold water. In it she was rubbing white cloth, rubbing almost desperately, her hands red from the cold. Charity's eyes asked a question.

'It's blood,' Ann said, 'On the sheet, and on my petticoat.'

'You look so cold,' Charity said. 'Why don't you just leave them to soak?'

'I've been cold all night,' Ann said. 'He took a blanket.'

'Shall I light the fire?'

Ann followed her dumbly to the hearth, where fuel was to hand, and when Charity had laid the kindling she bent and lit it from the tinder box. Only then did Charity venture to ask, 'Who took the blanket?'

'James.' Ann held her hands out to the flames, which as yet gave more illumination than warmth. 'He's gone to London.'

She pushed her hair back, and flinched. 'He hit me, on my head.' Already a greyness round her eye socket presaged a black eye. Suddenly she said, 'It was worse than that. He raped me. Such pain!' Then turning to Charity, 'But what can you know about the marriage bed?'

'Not the marriage bed,' Charity said. She shuddered, forcing herself to say, 'I know about rape.' And there, crouching together as the warmth of the fire built up, she began to tell Ann what she knew.

'Yes, pain.' She shook her head, remembering. 'It was my own fault. A troop of soldiers demanded lodgings in the farmhouse. My aunt had run off into the fields, and I wanted to see them. They crowded into the kitchen and I ran up the stairs, but they saw me.'

She reached for a faggot and arranged it in the fire.

'I didn't think it mattered that they'd seen me. I could hear my grandmother disputing with them and all the voices, so I stayed in my little bedroom.'

She fell silent. She felt as if she were there again, hearing the alarming noise building up below her. 'They drank all the ale there was in the house,' she said, and then said nothing for a long time.

At last Ann said 'And?'

Charity took a deep breath. 'They came upstairs, and the officer stood outside my bedroom door and told them where to go to sleep. And then he came into my room.'

She smiled for a moment. 'He was quite good looking. He took off his buff coat and cuddled me, and that was pleasant at first, so I let him. But then he put his tongue inside my mouth and it tasted of beer so that I retched. And then – oh Ann!'

Charity buried her face in her hands. When she spoke again it was barely above a whisper. 'He undressed and pulled off my shift and was on top of me on the bed. I screamed. No one came. They'd had to sleep in the shed. I'd think he was asleep, but then he'd do it again, pain after pain, worse every time. He did sleep in the end. At last I heard voices in the yard, and he woke up and grabbed me to start all over again. That's when I cried out. And Thomas rescued me.'

'Thomas?'

'My rescuer,' Charity said.

'But Thomas?'

'Thomas came and banged and banged on the door, and made the man get dressed. The man said he was going to kill me, and Thomas wrestled with him, and took his sword, and said there might be a battle, and made him go. I heard them leave with their horses.'

'But why was Thomas there at all?'

'They said he had some valuable load in his cart and the soldiers were escorting him.'

'And he brought you here after that?'

'Oh no. That was four years ago, when I was only twelve. Thomas just appeared this last summer, and they said I should go with him.'

'Four years! What did your people think about the rape?'

'I've never talked about it to anyone, till now. I felt so ashamed. If I hadn't ventured downstairs… if I hadn't enjoyed his cuddling… I've been over and over it in my head, over and over.'

159

'So you understand the pain. And from a stranger!'

'He just came, and went.'

'But I have to go on living with my husband.'

Charity put her hand over Ann's and they sat silently for a while. Light had begun to come in through the window, making the rush light in the back room dim by comparison.

'You're getting a black eye,' Charity said.

'Oh no! What will people say! My mother will have it all over the town. I'll need to say I tripped and caught my head on something.'

'Why did he hit you?'

Ann did not reply at once. It can't have been only because there was nothing for him to eat.

'He does get angry at times. I don't know why. He was angry when he came home, and then when there was no food he was angrier still. It's difficult knowing how to have food ready for him.'

Charity stood up. 'Have you any money? I'm hungry and we could buy some bread and then I must go home, or Abigail will wonder what has become of me.'

Thomas had spent a second night as the Kiffins' guest, for Thursday was filled with business, delivering to the store the Grocers' Company had set up, and gathering goods to carry to Farnham. James too, he imagined, had been doing business with William Kiffin and his leather selling friends, although the talk in the evening was more domestic.

'The first oranges are in from Spain,' Hanna had announced. James must also have made that discovery, for he handed Thomas a small basket of oranges saying 'Would you take these to Ann?' and then, almost apologetically, he added 'I'd be glad if you would see that all is well with her.'

Only a week away from home, Thomas thought as he rode the loaded cart out of London. What devotion! Yet there was something in James' manner which puzzled him.

Putney Heath reminded him of James' excited reaction on the journey into London when he saw the multitude of tents pitched there. 'It's the Army,' Thomas had told him, 'They've been here for several weeks. Must have mulked the whole neighbourhood of provisions by now.' It was as if James had suddenly come to life.

Thomas was home too late that evening to visit Ann, and he had much to do, with delivering some of his load, transferring other goods to the small cart and then with Hal's help seeing to the horses for the night. So it was Saturday morning when he went round to Church Lane and knocked at her door.

No one came, and he wondered if he had mistaken the cottage. He knew it was next to the bakery, and he noted the bakery with its unmistakable chimney. He knocked again, more loudly. A sound like something being dropped came from inside. And then Ann cautiously opened the door.

She looked utterly dishevelled, as if she had quickly pulled on a skirt over a shift, pushed her arms into a bodice and perched a cap on top of uncombed hair. She had wooden pattens on her feet (she must have dropped one as she came) and clutched a shawl around herself. 'Thomas,' she said.

'I've brought something for you from James,' he said. 'May I come in?'

Ann opened the door a little wider. 'I suppose you'd better,' she said.

The cottage was scarcely warmer than the chill outdoors, and she huddled onto a stool, tucking her feet up under her. Thomas remained standing.

'James bought these oranges for you,' he said, 'the first in from Spain. He asked me to bring them and to see how you are.'

'As well he might,' Ann muttered. 'Put the oranges in the cupboard, please.'

The cupboard had little in it. 'James sent you some money as well,' handing her a small bag of coins. She took it without a word. Thomas tried not to stare at her, she who was normally so neat and well dressed. Eventually he said, 'Are you unwell?'

'No.' Then Ann seemed to think a better answer was required and said, 'I was in bed. There wasn't much cause to get up, though I was cold. Can you please bring me the blanket James took?'

Thomas nodded. 'Your eye,' he said. 'How did you get a black eye?'

'Oh, I tripped, and…' She paused. Then she squared her shoulders and pulled the shawl more lightly round her. 'You might as well know,' she said. 'James hit me.'

So, Thomas thought, that temper of his extends to his wife. The oranges may be a peace offering.

'I'll fetch the blanket while you dress,' he said.

She took coins out of the bag he had brought her. 'Would you buy some bread at the same time?'

When he returned she looked more as she normally did, except for the black eye. She had some wet linen in a basket and was about to hang it up in the back yard. He helped her. Hurdles stacked against the privy wall aroused his curiosity.

'I want to keep hens,' Ann said. 'James bought me the hurdles but he's never put them up. It only needs a few posts, and somewhere to shut the hens at night.'

'Here's the bread,' Thomas said, 'and the change. I'll probably see you in church tomorrow.

Ann was not in church. She spent Sunday indoors, aware that she was using up the supply of fuel just to keep warm, alternating between terror that her mother would come to discover the reason for her absence, and resentment that she had not come to enquire after her health.

She stitched the shirt Betty had asked her to make for little Michael, that mischievous mother's pet who seemed to grow out of his clothes faster than new could be made. His older brothers used their clothes so roughly that little wear remained in them to be passed on. She sewed until the light failed and the fire subsided, when she went to bed.

So it was with some apprehension that she answered the knock on the door on the Monday morning, and relief to find Charity on her doorstep with little Simon in tow. Her relief was such that she embraced Charity warmly, and drew them both indoors.

'I was afraid you were my mother,' Ann said.

Charity laughed. 'Your mother is confined at home,' she said. 'She and some of the children have severe colds.'

'And she will be wrapping them up and feeding them tisanes and fussing,' Ann said. 'That has served me well, then.'

'Are you not concerned for them?' Charity asked.

'If you knew my mother...' Ann said. 'She'll soon be outdoors telling everyone how ill they've been, and catching

163

up with the gossip.'

Embarrassed, Charity said 'Your eye looks better. Just a little grey under it, scarcely noticeable.'

'But I'll stay indoors for a while, and finish my sewing.'

Simon had been holding himself close to Charity but now he began to investigate the room. Part of Ann's sewing was hanging over the edge of the table. Simon grabbed it and pulled. Ann dived forward to rescue needle, thread, scissors. Charity knelt down to try to release the garment from Simon's surprisingly strong grip. He protested and held on tightly, until a knock came at the door. He let go at once and went to the door, pressing his hands against the wood and looking up at the latch.

'We can't open the door with you in the way.' Charity scrambled to her feet and picked him up. Ann opened the door. And there was Thomas. Thomas! The few times she had seen him since she came here she had felt ill at ease, and this was no exception. Simon wriggled and protested at being held. Thomas looked at each of them in turn, taken aback. He addressed Ann.

'I've brought some posts for your hen run,' he said. 'Can I get round the outside to your back yard?'

'You'll have to come through the house,' Ann said.

He put a bag with a few tools in it on the floor while he carried through the posts. Simon promptly started investigating the bag's contents. 'Come Simon,' Charity said, 'You carry this hammer.'

Thomas paced the width of the hurdles, paced out a possible lay-out under Ann's direction, and began to drive in a corner post. Simon was everywhere underfoot, until Thomas said, 'Simon, you're a pest.' Then as he paused a new thought struck him. 'I'll leave the rest to James,' he said, putting his tools into their bag. 'He may want to complete it himself.'

'Not teaching him to finish things he should have started?' Ann said.

Thomas gave her a long look. 'You don't know my brother,' he said.

That angry man, Ann thought, unpredictable. Don't I know him? But there was no arguing with Thomas. Instead she offered him some ale, one item that they did keep in stock. She poured it and they sat round the table, Simon on the floor attempting to pull a faggot apart.

'Charity's been telling me how you rescued her after she was raped,' Ann said.

Charity gasped. She whispered 'Ann, that was between the two of us.'

'But Thomas knows all about it anyway,' Ann said. 'And people are saying it's a mystery why you went and fetched her here.'

'Let it remain a mystery,' Thomas said firmly. 'It is none of their business.'

'I told you.' Charity's quiet voice was vehement. 'My grandmother arranged for him to bring me here.'

'But it's like a story, the valiant prince rescuing the maiden, though I suppose after what happened you could not be called a maiden.'

Thomas looked away, embarrassed. Ann made her own interpretation. 'Did you desire Charity for yourself?'

Charity stood up, suddenly afraid. Might that actually be Thomas' reason for bringing her here? But she had hardly seen him since that alarming ride. He must be despising her.

Tears were welling up in her eyes. She needed to run, run away, run anywhere from these words. From Ann, no confidante. From Thomas, no rescuer it seemed but a betrayer. She as worthless as she feared.

She seized Simon and ran, ran with him, ran to the only safe place in this strange town, ran to Abigail.

Once inside the house Simon wriggled out of her hold and landed on the floor. She stood against the closed door, weeping and weeping, weeping as she had not wept since she was a child, since before the rape had shut down her emotions.

Abigail put her work aside. 'Charity, dear one,' she said, attempting to hold her as Phoebe would have done. Charity tensed, one arm tightly round herself, unworthy of affection. She could not restrain her sobs.

Simon toddled up. He put his hand on Charity's thigh and looking up at her said 'Stop crying now.' He sounded so like Abigail when she soothed him, that in spite of herself Charity had to smile. 'Dear Simon,' she said. She picked him up and he gently tried to wipe her tears with his soft hand.

She looked at Abigail through bleary eyes. 'I thought Ann was a friend,' was all the explanation she could manage. 'And Thomas…

'Thomas is a good man,' Abigail said. 'He is shy of you.

Thomas had returned to London with the next week's load of grain, and they sat together round the Kiffins' meal table. He and James would be off early next morning for his return trip.

'You'll be back with your bride!' Hanna said.

James grunted. Hanna and William exchanged glances.

'Little seems to have been resolved at Putney,' William said.

'Motions for universal suffrage, opposition to that; motions for addresses to the King, or no more addresses to the King. They want General Fairfax to ask Parliament to postpone approaching the King until the Army Council has made its own recommendations. One wonders who wields the power, Parliament or the Army.'

'John Lilburne must be frustrated,' Hanna said, 'Hearing everything at second hand and not able to take part.'

'I bought a copy of *An Agreement of the People*,' James said. 'It was published yesterday, so now we can properly know what is put forward.'

William smiled. 'Good reading matter for your journey home, if the way is not too rutted.'

'Aren't you excited, to be going home?' Hanna asked.

James leant his head against his hand, and looked into his almost empty goblet. This week in London had filled his thoughts, and only sometimes, as he walked between places, did home come into them. Excited? He shrugged.

'I wish I knew Ann,' Hanna said. 'Do tell me about her.'

It was a while before James responded, slowly.

'She's well dressed, a seamstress. She sews a lot. Her father is the local woollen draper; prosperous, a Burgess.'

Hanna waited.

'She's not interested in what's going on – I mean she won't listen if I read her *"An Agreement of the People"*.'

'Might she read it herself?'

'I'm not sure that she can read. Though my mother did write her a list of the provisions she should lay in. And then, although I give her money, she never seems to have things by.

'Housekeeping is an art in itself,' Hanna said.

'James,' William said, 'Did you tell your brother about the encounter we had last Sunday? With Walter Hutchcroft, John Woodbridge's man?'

'Ah. No.' James turned to Thomas. 'This man,' he said, 'is from the New World. He's been trying to trace his daughter. Lived on a farm Oxford way.'

'Quite hard to follow his tale,' William said. 'He was almost incoherent with excitement, though he seems now to have lost the trail.'

'Wasn't it,' James turned to William, 'Wasn't it our surname which made a sort of connexion?'

'Mannory. Yes. Something about the girl's grandmother. The girl wasn't at the farm any more, he said. She had been sent away, but he didn't know whither.'

Thomas stood up. 'Do you know where these men are lodging? I must talk with them.'

'It's too late now,' William said. 'I'll arrange for you to meet with them next week.'

Thomas excused himself and went to bed. James turned back to his hosts. 'You two,' he said. 'You two, have you always been this contented?'

William looked at Hanna. 'Are we?' he said.

'You know of some of the conflicts and uncertainties around us,' Hanna said.

'And blessings, certainly as far as commerce is concerned,' William added.

'You do seem to have flourished,' James said.

'Only recently. We were quite poor when we first married.'

'And it was discontent,' William said, 'discontent with trade as it then was, that first prompted me to set up trade with

Amsterdam.'

'We would be more contented if we had a son,' Hanna said.

'But,' James searched for words, 'contented with each other.'

William and Hanna exchanged a long look.

'Ten years we've been married,' William said. 'Time to learn each other,' he smiled suddenly, 'though I've still a lot to learn.'

'That's love, isn't it. Learning to understand each other.'

'Love tempering lust.'

'You seem so contented,' James said.

'Contented with each other?' William said. 'Yes.'

Back in Farnham James dawdled as Thomas unharnessed his horses and settled them for the night. He helped him stow what needed to be delivered during the coming week, until Thomas said, 'Well, that's it for tonight. Thanks for your help,' and locked up.

The November evening was dark. James walked slowly over the cobbles up Church Lane. Then, as he passed the bakery, he saw there was a light in the cottage window, a wax candle no less. Wondering, he opened the door.

The table was clean and laid. A low fire was keeping their black cauldron simmering, suspended from the hook above it. Ann stood uncertainly beside the hearth as he entered.

'The candle...,' he said.

'Please don't be angry,' Ann blurted out. 'About the expense. It was intended as a welcome.'

'A welcome it is,' James said, without moving. Ann gestured to the table.

'You must be hungry after your journey. Please do eat.'

She scooped food out of the cauldron, root vegetables

and big pieces of meat. The meat fell off the bone as his fork touched it, delicious.

'It's rabbit,' Ann said. 'They had some in the market. I had not money for beef, and everyone says beef has become very expensive.' She helped herself to a portion.

James watched her as they ate. Something about her reminded him of that apprentice he had beaten in the spring. Cautious. Afraid even. When she turned her head the light caught the remains of bruising under one eye.

She finished eating and looked up, but not at him. 'Thomas brought some posts for my hen run,' she said. 'But he reckoned you might be angry if he erected it himself, so he just stacked them. Oh, he did drive in one.' Then as an afterthought she added, 'Thank you for the oranges… and the money.'

James pondered this as he wiped the last of the food out of his bowl with a crust of bread. Now when he looked up at her, she was looking directly at him, with nothing more to say but an expression which stirred his desire for her. An expression which could be one of desire for him.

'Have you had enough to eat?' She lifted the pot off its hook and rested it in the cool part of the hearth. She gathered plates and cutlery and carried them to the sink. He stood up and followed her, ducking under the staircase until he stood behind her at the sink. She did not move. He touched her neck where strands of hair had strayed from under her cap. The hair was silky and soft, faintly auburn in the dim light. He stroked her skin, and felt a kind of shudder run through her. Go slowly. Let love temper lust.

He turned her towards himself. Such a pretty face. He ran his finger gently over each cheek. Under one eye the cheek was discoloured, slightly puffy. With an effort he said, 'I'm sorry I hurt you.'

Never before in his life had he apologised for anything. He did not know what to expect in response. Not, perhaps, the silence which greeted it. She turned away, and said, 'What's done is done.'

A barrier had reared between them. A barrier his instinct was to storm. His apology had yielded nothing. He felt humiliated. Yet he had seen that she desired him. He drew her to him but she said 'Not tonight, James,' and he knew he must not repeat the violence he had done her last time.

Chapter 13 - Corkbush

A bigail woke with a start a week later as dawn was no more than a hint, woken by the clatter of hooves in the street below, the sound of horses ridden purposefully. She scrambled out of bed to look through the window.

She glimpsed them as they passed the last of the houses and were urged to a canter.

'What are you doing this cold morning?' Ralph asked sleepily from the warmth of the bed.

'A party of horsemen,' Abigail said, 'Four or five of them. Heading out towards Alton. Looked to be in haste. Why so early and why in such a hurry?'

Even earlier, Thomas set out for London, determined to give himself time once there to talk with these men from the New World. William Kiffin had been as good as his word and arranged for him to go to their lodgings that evening. They sat down together, he, John Woodbridge and Walter Hutchcroft. Woodbridge took initial command of the conversation.

'We have come from Massachusetts in the New World where we are settled. Settled a good many years now. Walter Hutchcroft came over with me as an indentured servant, but he has been my general factotum long since. I wouldn't want to do without him. I understand you are somehow connected with Pastor Kiffin.'

'I carry goods to London weekly,' Thomas said. 'My brother deals in fine skins and I deliver them to Master Kiffin. He is a freeman of the Leatherworkers Company.'

'A man of many interests it seems,' Woodbridge said, 'and wide acquaintance.'

'He has been helpful and hospitable to my brother and me,' Thomas said.

'To business, then,' Woodbridge said. 'Walter has been trying to trace the daughter he has never known. I am not clear how you or your brother feature in the story.'

'It was the name,' Walter said. 'Let me tell you what I know so far,' and he launched into a torrent of words. Once he had overcome his initial excitement, he more slowly described the farmhouse where he had left his wife, described the antagonistic grandmother, Margie the sister-in-law, the surroundings and location. The more he said, the more recognisable it became. Reluctantly, Thomas had to concede that Walter might indeed be Charity's father. 'Let it remain a mystery' he had said to Ann, but here was a mystery he could not leave unchallenged. One question remained.

'Do you know what they called your daughter?' he said.

'Charity! That's what they called her. The Reverend Woodbridge told me her name when he wrote about her mother's death. Charity. It is she I am seeking.'

Thomas said nothing. He thought of Charity, of how little he knew about her, of how little he actually knew her, except for her horrified distress at Ann's betrayal and conjecture. This seemingly timid girl, suddenly to have a father. Must he be the one to tell her about him? He could not imagine how he would go about it.

Woodbridge and Walter were looking expectantly at him. 'Charity,' he said. 'I think I know where she is.'

He swallowed, making a decision. 'I will see what I can do. Then perhaps, if your claim proves to be correct, perhaps it can be arranged for you to meet.'

It had been an eventful week. The best news was that John Lilburne had been released from the Tower on bail. He called on the Kiffins to thank William for helping to find lodgings for him and his family. They welcomed him warmly, and sat down to hear his latest news.

'You know about the King of course,' Lilburne said, 'his escape from Hampton Court Palace?'

'Escape?' William said. 'King Charles gave me his word that he would not attempt to escape the Palace.'

'Blame his counsellors if you like. They've always been blamed for the king's shortcomings.'

'Where did he go?'

'Through Windsor forest in the night, and changed horses at Alton and on to Southampton. His companions must have organised it.'

'I'm surprised he didn't head for Dover and cross to France,' William said.

'Maybe they got lost in the dark. At all events he has landed up on the Isle of Wight.'

'What a betrayal!' William sighed. 'Was I foolish to believe he was a man of his word?'

'I had been thinking monarchy a better alternative to having such as Cromwell in power, but that depends so much on the monarch as a man. And this King as a man seems to be devious and outright dishonest.'

Hanna called a servant to bring them some ale.

'And what of the debates at Putney?' William asked as they drank. 'Did Rainsborough tell you more?'

'The whole proceedings frustrated him. They passed a motion for manhood suffrage, with just the exception of servants and beggars, and then a day or so later another motion reversed it. Cromwell said it would tend to anarchy. Another thing; some favoured negotiating with the King, some against.'

'It's hard to know which is right,' William said.

'Rainsborough told me that nothing was resolved. The Council was disbanded. Officers and agents were sent back to their regiments with the promise of a rendezvous. There's a new council now, just officers. Farewell democracy!'

'I hear that the House of Commons has denounced *The Agreement of the People* and wants to find out who wrote it.'

'It's a powerful document. Unpopular with those in power because of its demands for the reform of Parliament, although it's all for the central authority of Parliament itself.'

'And what of the rendezvous?'

'It was only a part rendezvous. You know the saying "divide and rule". Just three regiments of foot and three of cavalry were ordered to attend.'

'And you?'

'Young Wildman and I heard it was to be at Corkbush Field, not far from the present Army headquarters at Hertford. So we went along. We couldn't get onto the Field with all the milling around, but we had a pretty good view.'

'I haven't understood why there was a rendezvous at all,' Hanna said.

'The grandees wanted the soldiers, both officers and men, to take an oath of loyalty to General Fairfax and the Army

Council, and to accept *The Heads of the Proposals*. That's the paper Fairfax and Ireton prepared, and watered down too after showing it to the King. The bait was an assurance of full payment of their arrears of pay.'

'Loyalty to the Army Council?' William said. 'But it's Parliament that votes to pay.'

'And somehow they linked back pay and the oath of loyalty. No oath, no pay.'

'Bribery?' Hanna said.

'Well, when we got there a couple of officers were haranguing the soldiers, inciting them against General Fairfax – Fairfax, who has led them faithfully through battles, and has begged Parliament to raise funds for their pay. They were promptly arrested, but others were distributing copies of *The Agreement of the People*. So things were pretty tense when suddenly two other regiments, against orders, appeared. One of them was my brother Robert's regiment. The soldiers had driven away most of their officers, some with stones, and marched in wearing copies of the *Agreement* in their hatbands.'

He held out his tankard for more ale.

'Fairfax talked with them and brought them round – they do respect him – all except my brother Robert's regiment. They kept shouting until Cromwell rode among them with drawn sword in his hand.'

'That was brave!' Hanna said.

'He and his men arrested the evident ringleaders, and had one Private shot on the spot as an example. Coming to Corkbush contrary to orders was mutiny'

'So it all fizzled out,' William said.

'At least Rainsborough approached Fairfax and presented him with a copy of *The Agreement of the People* in the name of the soldiery.'

'Poor man!' Hanna said. 'General Fairfax I mean. He must feel in a great dilemma.'

'He's loved by the soldiers,' Lilburne said, 'and he seemed to calm them and reassure them. After such firm action with the rabble rousers, maybe the other two rendezvous planned will be less eventful. If they get their pay, that is.'

'Thinking of Rainsborough,' Lilburne went on, 'Members of the House of Commons can't make up their minds about him. First they appointed him to be Vice-Admiral of the Navy, which he took to mean they wanted him out of the way. And then others were afraid he'd spread his Leveller convictions among the sailors, and pulled back. So Rainsborough doesn't know where he stands.'

'If only Parliament would vote to pay the soldiers what they are owed, they'd happily disband go home., wouldn't they?' William said.

'Some at least,' Lilburne said disconsolately. 'Others look like being sent to Ireland. And rumour has it that the King keeps negotiating with the Scots, and even with some Irish, trying to gain support.'

William sighed. 'God preserve us from more war,'

Whether it was because of these oaths; or because of the promise of pay; or because the Army joined in a whole day of earnest prayer at Windsor; or because of the business of simply living in winter time; or because of Fairfax's reassurances, political activity in the Army simmered down.

Not so among Royalist sympathisers. Not so in pamphlet production. Not so among civilian Leveller supporters, led tirelessly by John Lilburne. Dedicated committees regularly met, often addressed by him, and thousands of pamphlets circulated.

But in January, moles attended an apparently insignificant meeting in Wapping. Thought to be "scruplers", come to have their questions and "scruples" addressed by Lilburne and Wildman, they sat through the meeting with growing excitement. No sooner had it ended than they rushed off to the House of Commons, spouting a sometimes inaccurate but generally incriminating account of all that they had witnessed.

Once again John Lilburne, and this time John Wildman as well, were imprisoned, but not before Lilburne's long defence had been courteously heard. The Wapping meeting's emphasis, he reiterated, had been on preserving the interest and being of the House of Commons. Wildman also made his case, and the Commons debated long while the two men awaited their decision in a side room.

Wildman was sent to the Fleet prison. Lilburne was allowed a day's grace to spend with his family. When he reported back to the House the next day to give himself up, a huge crowd of supporters was there ahead of him. Nothing daunted he stood and preached law and justice, and the illegality of arresting him without a legal warrant, until the soldiers sent to arrest him called for reinforcements. Swords flashed, and only the indefatigable Elizabeth Lilburne interposing herself prevented bloodshed.

To dodge the crowds, the escort took Lilburne to the Tower of London by water.

Whether in the Tower or at liberty, nothing restrained Lilburne's pen, and his writings found immediate publication and dispersal.

Around the country, Royalist sympathies were building up.

Chapter 14 - Orphans

Christmas had passed almost without notice, although the ban on celebrating it caused such rioting in Kent and Essex that much damage was done and the Army was called in to quell the chaos. But in Farnham few people bothered to bring in the traditional fir branches to decorate their houses. Life continued much as normal, and Thomas realised that weeks had gone by since Walter Hutchcroft had told him of his search. He might wait indefinitely for a chance opportunity to talk with Charity.

So with some trepidation he knocked at the Attfields' door one February morning. Ralph and Abigail were working at their bench, and he chatted nervously with them, discussing some of the conflicting loyalties that newsbooks recounted, talking of the weather and of trade. Eventually he pulled himself together and asked if he could speak with Charity.

'Surely,' Abigail said. 'You'll find her in the back room. She manages to look after Simon at the same time as preparing food.'

She was sitting at the table with Simon on her knee, drawing on a scrap of paper with a piece of charcoal. Thomas was reluctant to intrude on this comfortable scene. He sat down on a stool to be on a level with them.

'Charity,' he said at last, 'I need to talk with you.' Then seeing her alarmed expression he said, 'I've been told something which concerns you and your family.'

'Not death?' she exclaimed. 'What have you heard?'

'I've heard nothing about your people at the farm,' Thomas said.

Charity drew a meaningless squiggle on the paper. Simon rubbed his hand on the charcoal, and inspected the mark on his palm. Thomas knew he must be direct.

'You know I carry regularly to London?' he said. 'Through our contact there I was introduced to someone who has come over the ocean from the New World. He is seeking a daughter he has never met. From what he has told me, it seems possible that you may be that daughter.'

'Me?' Charity clutched Simon so hard that he protested. 'From the New World?'

'From Massachusetts,' Thomas said.

'That's where they used to tell me my father went, and never came back.'

'Would the name Walter Hutchcroft mean anything to you?'

'Hutchcroft? Why that is my surname!'

Thomas smiled at her. 'I only ever knew you as Charity,' he said. Then he told her what Walter had related, and how he had become convinced that he was describing the farm and family where she had been raised. 'But I didn't know, I don't know, how you would receive this, so I have taken a while to come and tell you. Cowardly I suppose.'

Charity said slowly, 'My grandmother spoke of him only to condemn. He married my mother in a rush. They were very young. Grandmother called him hasty and irresponsible.'

'He is certainly quick. And eager.' Thomas said. 'His employer values him, said he couldn't do without him. More like a friend than a servant.'

Charity put Simon down and brushed her apron. 'I don't know what to think,' she said.

Throughout the winter Charity had been going down Church Lane only when Abigail asked her to go and buy bread. Quickly in and out of the bakery, she would hurry back, thankful not to have encountered Ann. On Sundays she often asked to stay behind and mind Simon. On the occasions when she went to church she would sit in an unobtrusive corner, and leave the moment the service was over. Ralph and Abigail never questioned her nor required her to be with them. She sensed that they knew the gossip which had spread about her.

Simon's cry of 'Walk!' she countered easily on cold or wet days. Other days she led him up towards the Castle, the deer park and the hop fields. He lagged on the steep climb up out of the town, and the fields were often muddy. Then they would run back down the hill, she sometimes ahead so that she could catch him and swing him round, sometimes hand in hand together. Yet February had some warm even spring-like days, tempting her to extend their range.

They walked along above the hop fields and the clay pits until they reached the brickworks. Men were wire-cutting bricks and stacking them, in preparation for the next firing. Ahead, she saw Thomas' small cart, with 'Thomas Mannory Carrier' painted on its side and the little old cob waiting patiently, her muzzle in a nosebag of hay.

Hal sauntered over with 'Hullo you!', his habitual greeting to Simon as if he didn't have a name. 'You've had a good climb from home,' turning to Charity.

'We often venture into the deer park,' Charity said, 'but

today I thought we'd try this way. It's very muddy.'

'I'll give you a ride back down if you like,' Hal said, 'when they've finished loading.' He perched on a pile of bricks and gestured to her to sit beside him.

'Two orphans in a row,' he said cheerfully, 'or rather Abigail says you are an orphan, and I am in a way.'

Charity looked at him, waiting for more.

'My mother died when I was six or seven,' he said. 'Tanner Mannory is said to have fathered me, so I'm only a partial orphan.'

'Partial orphan,' Charity repeated. 'My mother died when I was a baby,' she said. 'My father went away before I was born. And now...'

Hal sat quietly, gazing past the brick sheds to the greening fields beyond, up and up through the parkland, as if ignoring her half finished sentence. 'Ralph Attfield became like a father to me. I was his paddy boy during the war. I took care of his horses.'

He began to tell her about the battle of Cropredy, how he had searched among wounded and dying men until he had found him, pinned under his dead horse, his leg broken, his face covered in blood.

'I feared he was dead,' he said, 'and all the time he was in fever, we feared he was dying.'

'So you weren't alone?' Charity said.

'No, in Mother Metcalfe's cottage.' But near death and dread of death were not what he had set out to say, nor to tell the tale. 'It was just that Mother Metcalfe got me to talk about my mother's death. To grieve I suppose. I found my mother in a pool of blood, and the dead baby too, and then the Mannorys whisked me away and never talked about it. They just took me in and that was that. Mother Metcalfe's listening was healing.'

Charity watched Simon playing in the mud, and let him do it. She was picturing her grandfather, that dear inoffensive loving farmer, willingly dominated by his adored wife.

'I'd like to have talked with my grandfather,' she said, 'but he died.'

She shifted her position on the hard angular bricks.

'Hal,' she said into the silence. 'Hal, may I tell you something?'

'If you would like to,' Hal said.

'When Thomas was in London, he met a man who thinks he is my father. He has talked with Thomas. Thomas can't have made it up. So much of what the man told him sounds true. Thomas said I'm to let him know when I'm ready for the man to hear that I may be his daughter. I keep worrying about it.'

'Have you met him?' Hal asked.

'No, I haven't, and I keep putting off doing anything about it.'

'Imagine,' Hal said slowly, 'what it would mean to him to know you; for his daughter to be real for him. And wouldn't you like to know your father?'

'It's just that my grandmother spoke so ill of him. She almost blamed him for my mother's death.'

'You will only know for sure when you have met him.' Hal looked away, up the hill again, before he said, 'It would be good to be sure of who your father is. I would like that.'

'Didn't you say that Master Mannory is your father?' Charity said.

'It's what I have been led to believe. But then I was talking to Abe Trussler, and he threw at me that he could well be my father. Because he often had my mother, in lieu of rent for that cottage we lived in.'

He looked at Charity, trying to gauge her reaction. 'She had to earn money somehow,' he said. 'Master Mannory was one of the men who went to her. Just once, I'm told.'

'If I meet this man, at least I could know, one way or the other,' she said.

At that moment Simon stood up, toddled over to them and planted muddy hands in Charity's lap. 'Made a mess,' he said. He was mud all over, on hands feet, legs, arms and face. He wiped his hands vigorously on Charity's apron. 'Oh Simon!' she giggled.

'See how you are loved!' Hal said. Mud notwithstanding, he picked Simon up. 'We'll give you a ride in the cart,' he said.

'Now that the days are longer,' Ralph said in March, 'I think I should ride to Petersfield and find out what has become of my inheritance there.'

'Why not take Hal with you?' Abigail said. 'You might be able to arrange an apprenticeship for him somewhere along the way.'

So he hired two horses and together they set out early, following the lanes which Ralph remembered from his horse dealing days.

'Good to be on a horse again,' he said.

First the way led through the forest which Hal knew well, for he and Thomas often went there to collect the oak bark from which tannin was extracted for tanning. Then there was open heathland, until more forest. Then at last onto chalk land, undulating and green, and the going was easier.

Hal looked across at Ralph who was restlessly shifting his position on the saddle. 'Your leg paining you?' he asked.

'A little,' Ralph said. 'It's so long since I was in the saddle.'

'Should we dismount and rest?'

'If I dismounted now I'd be hard put to mount again. No, I'll not give up now. We'll soon be there.'

They stabled the horses at the White Hart Inn, paid for hay for them and went out into the square. The place was thronged, for it was market day. Ralph was limping towards the Borough Hall, Hal anxiously beside him, when a shout stopped them.

'Attfield! Is it you, Ralph Attfield?'

Ralph turned towards a weather-beaten man much his own age. 'Jim! Jim Hosier!' and almost simultaneously they both said 'What are you doing here?'

'Well, I live here,' Jim said. 'But you, I haven't seen you in years.'

'I was out of the war after the battle at Cropredy.'

'And I when they created the New Model Army.'

'You remember Hal, who was my paddy boy in the Army?'

'Hal! Yes, the lad with a way with horses. Come, we surely have a deal to tell each other. Can you sit for a while?'

They found a bench, and talked as old soldiers do, recalling skirmishes and battles, dwelling less on the tedious trailing over the country, the uncomfortable quarters, the lost comrades.

'Had the Cropredy battle not disabled me, I could have joined the New Model Army,' Ralph said. 'But you...'

'Sir William Waller lost his regiment of horse when the New Model Army was set up. He wasn't given a command in that. I didn't want to serve under anyone else,' Jim said.

'So you went back to being his coachman?'

'You haven't heard what happened to him?' Jim said. 'After the fighting ended, Parliament sent him and a couple of other Members of Parliament to arrange things with the Army. But the Army would have none of it. Then the Independent party in the House of Commons took against the prominent Presbyterian members and excluded them from the House. Sir William was one of them.' Hal kept watching closely, trying to keep up.

'After that,' Jim said, 'it looked as if Parliament and the City of London might be at war, don't ask me why. The City called on Sir William, along with two others excluded from Parliament, to mobilise the City's militia.'

He turned to Hal. 'You see there's this division between Presbyterians and Independents. Sir William is staunchly Presbyterian, and I understand the Army mostly favours the Independents.'

'And did they fight?' Hal asked.

'No, it was patched up. The long and the short of it is that Sir William fled the country. I hear that he and Lady Waller with their children and the other Generals are lodging in the Netherlands.'

'No coach and no coachman,' Ralph said.

'The coach went a long time ago,' Jim said. 'Poor man. Remember when he was acclaimed as William the Conqueror? And now in exile.'

Now Jim wanted to hear how Ralph had fared, and about the harness making trade he had mentioned in passing.

'Hal saved my life when I was wounded,' Ralph said, 'and we learnt harness making from the old woman he found to nurse me. I've been trying to put Hal as apprentice to a horse collar maker, so that we could work alongside. Might you know of anyone looking for an apprentice?'

'But Hal should be with horses!' Jim exclaimed. 'I've never forgotten, Hal, the way you handled our horses when we were billeted at the Tanyard, after we took Farnham Castle. You have a gift which should not be wasted.'

'I look after Thomas' three horses,' Hal said quietly. 'Thomas is a carter.'

'You could take to horse dealing like Ralph did,' Jim said. 'Every day all year with horses!'

Ralph and Hal exchanged a long look.

'Or a stud.' Jim was warming to his topic. 'The war killed so many horses, they're in demand now.'

'That would require capital,' Ralph said, dismissing further discussion.

'The reason I came over today,' he said, 'is to track down a small property I inherited here. At least I suppose I still have it. I need to see the Coroner and find out if he knows anything about it.'

He stood up. 'You'd best wait here for me,' he said to Hal, before weaving his way lamely through the market stalls to the Borough Hall.

Hal turned to Jim. 'A stud?' he said.

'I run a small scale stud,' Jim said. 'Started off with a young stallion, and people began to bring their mares to be served. Acquired a few mares. It's rearing the foals that I most enjoy.'

'What a life!' Hal's eyes were alight.

'You have to remember it's a business,' Jim said. 'Save all you can and buy judiciously.'

They sat in silence then, watching the market activity. Ralph was not gone long.

'Just a couple of fields,' he reported, 'as I thought. There may be rent owed to me. I'd like to sell them and buy the house I'm renting in Farnham.'

Jim wanted to know about those fields. He listened carefully as Ralph explained their location. Then he insisted on them following him to inspect them.

'Yes, those are the fields,' Ralph said.

Jim chuckled. 'I reckon,' he said, 'that it is I who owes you rent for them. And you say you want to sell them?'

Never one to let the grass grow under his feet, Ralph quickly set things in motion to sell his fields to Jim. Only days after his visit to Petersfield he asked Charity to take a letter to the Bush Inn to be dispatched to him. It was early in the day, chilly, and she hurried to carry out the request.

A man was standing in the courtyard. He stretched his arms and shook his head, shaking off the frowstiness of sleep with the sharp morning air. Hurrying to the Inn door, Charity scarcely noticed him except that as she went inside she heard him shout 'Martha!'

She delivered the letter and came out again, slightly surprised that there was no woman in the courtyard to whom he might have been calling. But he was still there. He must have been waiting for her to come out of the Inn again, for he rushed up to her and seized her hands. She pulled back.

'Forgive me,' he said, burying his face in his own hands. When he looked up again there were tears in his eyes. 'You are Charity, are you not?' he said.

'Why yes, that is my name,' she said.

'I thought when I saw you that you were my dear wife, Martha,' he said. 'You are so exactly as I remember her. Young and dainty and......' he choked a sob. 'Are you truly Charity? Charity Hutchcroft?'

Charity nodded.

'Then sweet Charity, I believe you are my daughter.'

'But who are you?' Charity asked, cautious at this display of emotion.

'Walter. Walter Hutchcroft. Come from Massachusetts, and looking to find you. I saw Thomas Mannory yesterday who told me you were willing to meet me, so I straightway hired a horse and arrived here late last evening. Oh Charity! What it means to meet you in person, better by far than all my imaginings!'

Charity looked around her, for people had begun to come and go into the Inn.

'Let me take you to what is now my home,' she said. 'This is no place to be talking.'

Little work was done that day. Ralph and Abigail had known nothing of Thomas' meetings with Walter, for he had considered them totally confidential. He had even avoided mentioning these to William and Hanna, who respected his privacy. And James had seemed hardly interested. So there was much ground to cover, relationships to be explained. More than once Walter was on the cusp of embracing Charity, but something about her held him back.

'We lived near Stanton Fitzwarren, only a short way from the farm. Your grandparents' farm I mean. My folk were tenant farmers locally. We young people met often. Reverend John Woodbridge, the Rector, had some of us together for instruction, reading and mathematics and so on. His son, John, and I became good friends.'

'Where is Stanton Fitzwarren?' Ralph asked.

'Near the road to Oxford,' Walter said.

Abigail turned to Ralph. 'Thomas told us he was thereabouts because he was on his way to Oxford from Bath, remember?' she said.

'Not at my family farm?' Walter said

'No, it was...' Abigail shook her head.

Very quietly Charity said, 'During the fighting. Soldiers came to our farm, and.....and Thomas protected me.'

'I'll need to hear more about that,' Walter said. 'Our own story is that John Woodbridge, the younger that is, fell foul of church authorities. As indeed have some of his relatives. He refused to take the oath of uniformity so he had to leave Oxford University. He carried on his studies at home, which is where we got to know each other better.'

'But I understood you came from the New World,' Ralph said.

'We emigrated there when Massachusetts was first opened up,' Walter said. 'Woodbridge kindly took me as his indentured servant, and a servant of one sort or another he certainly needed. I can tell you it was a rough life to start with. Shiploads kept arriving, had to build themselves shacks as fast as they could. That's where I perfected my carpentry. Rich folk such as the governor employed craftsmen like me to build themselves good big houses. No change there from society in the Old World.'

'That was the wonder of the New Model Army as I've heard,' Ralph said. 'Promotion, leadership, was on proven qualities. Not on high birth.'

'Woodbridges have been clergymen for generations,' Walter said. 'John's employment in the New World was already arranged. Town clerk to the magistrates.'

'So settlers didn't delay in setting up government and courts?' Ralph said.

'Far from it. Offices and a meeting house for worship came even before houses.'

'Where does Charity come into this story?' Abigail asked.

'Ah!' A tender look came into Walter's eyes. 'Martha and I were sweethearts. She loved the idea, the adventure, of moving away to the New World. But we needed to marry, quickly. And then from all I'd heard I thought it unwise to take her across the ocean either before or soon after the babe was to be born. Too great a responsibility.'

'A risk for her,' Abigail said.

'Exactly. Many men who came over with us, sent for their wives later on, once they were settled. But my lovely Martha did not live to follow me.'

His flow of words dried up. He gazed at Charity so intently that she looked down, away, out through the window, anywhere to avoid his eyes.

'You look so like her,' he said, addressing her alone.

'I doubt I am adventurous.'

'Living under that grandmother of yours, perhaps you have had no chance,' he said. 'By and by, I'll tell you about the wonders of the New World.'

Abigail cobbled together a meal for the four of them. 'Will you be long in Farnham?' she asked.

'I may pass through any number of times,' Walter said.

'Master Woodbridge would prefer to be within easy reach of the Isle of Wight where King Charles is lodged, and Farnham is a good staging place for the journey there. But tonight he will be expecting me back with him in London.'

As soon as they finished eating he stood up to take his leave. 'Thank you for your kind hospitality and welcome,' he said to Ralph and Abigail. 'And Charity. What joy to find you, dear daughter! I long to know you better,' and spreading his arms he wrapped her in a big embrace, awkward because she scarcely yielded to its warmth.

Chapter 15 - Easter

'Soon be Easter time,' Thomas said cheerfully as he stood waiting for Piggott to pay him for the last month's carting.

'Parliament has put an end to that,' Piggott said.

'An end to Easter?' Thomas could not believe it.

'The Book of Common Prayer with all its religious observance is not to be used any more. The Presbyterian book is the one to be used.'

'They went and abolished Christmas,' Thomas said, 'and now Easter?'

'The Papist church tried to Christianise the pagan mid-winter festivals by setting up Christmas, and the pagan element persists.'

'What, bringing in greenery and cheering up the darkest day of the year?'

'And eating and drinking and singing and begging,' Piggott said.

'Some of the songs tell the Christmas story,' Thomas said.

'And most of them don't. They laud drinking. Think of "Wassail". And it is very unlikely that Jesus was actually born in mid-winter. What Roman Emperor or any ruler would command a census for mid-winter? Most probably the census was soon after harvest when the weather was clement and the main work finished for the year. I've studied the Biblical feasts. The feast of booths, of Tabernacles, at the end of harvest would be the time when Jesus took on the "tent" of humanity, being born as a man.'

'Thanks for the sermon, Sir,' Thomas said. 'They rioted in

Kent because Christmas was forbidden. Will there be rioting in favour of Easter?'

'We shall of course recall the resurrection,' Piggott said solemnly. 'It is designated as a day for recreation.'

'Dancing on the meadow, the maypole and sports and things?' Thomas said. 'And songs? What about, (he started to sing) "Summer is a coming in, loudly sing cuckoo, groweth seed and bloweth mead and springs the wood anew"?'

'An unedifying song, and certainly not dancing.' Piggott counted out the money owed and put it in a bag.

On his way back Thomas called in on Ralph and Abigail.

'Honestly,' he said. Hal happened to be there, and Charity and Simon too of course. 'Honestly, these Puritans want to take all the fun out of life.'

They looked up, surprised at his unusual vehemence.

'First of all they abolish Christmas, and now they're doing the same for Easter. Mister Piggott says it's to be a day of recreation, but no dancing and I wonder if even ale will be allowed. He says that's all pagan or Popish.'

'He's a prominent Burgess,' Abigail said. 'It does sound rather bleak, as if they're trying to make people good by passing laws.'

'You can't legislate for people to be good if they prefer otherwise,' Ralph said. 'No one can control another's virtue.'

'And who's to say dancing or singing aren't good?' Abigail said. 'I suppose there'll be a service of some sort on Easter Sunday.'

'Which we'll be obliged by law to attend,' Thomas said.

'When we were at Cropredy,' Ralph said, 'people used to

come to the house for what they called a Conventicle. We've talked about it before. There'd be no reason why we should not gather here to pray and hear the word of God. Not to interfere with our obligations to attend the parish church – a different day of the week.'

'Who would lead such a meeting?' Thomas asked. 'Would you?'

'It doesn't necessarily need a leader,' Ralph said. 'It depends on how in harmony people are, and hearing the Holy Spirit's leading.'

'I reckon you do need a leader,' Abigail said. 'Someone with discernment.'

'Young Billie Bicknell, Joan's brother, is studying theology at University,' Thomas said. 'He might be drawn in.'

'You think it's a good idea then?' Ralph asked.

'Give it a try. We've a Bible between us I presume, and we can read or, (catching sight of Charity and wondering momentarily if she could read) or listen.'

Hal's eyes were shining. 'That would be wonderful! I learnt so much from those Conventicles.'

'Don't approach young Bicknell for the time being,' Ralph said. 'Small meetings such as this can get into trouble. They're suspect. No point in courting imprisonment.'

'I have an early start every Thursday,' Thomas said, 'So could it be earlier in the week?'

'Tuesday evenings then?' Abigail said.

Betty Gary could scarcely contain herself through the Lenten Sunday service until she could tell the latest news. A knot of women gathered round her in the church porch, blocking the way out. However, she was not about to give her news to all and sundry, so she beckoned to the group to follow her outside where they formed a little listening huddle.

'My servant girl,' Betty began, 'is friendly with one of the house servants at the Bush.' She paused for effect. 'She told my girl that a famous person spent the night at the Inn.' Another pause. 'Someone recognised him. No less than General Oliver Cromwell!'

A gasp went round the group.

'No one seems to know why he was there,' Betty said. 'He ordered fuel and ale, and a man came and sat with him. A Hampshire gentleman.'

'He rode in,' one woman trumped her. 'My husband stabled his horses for him. His servant didn't know why he had come to Farnham.'

'Oh! But I do!' a stout young woman said. 'I carried in the ale they'd ordered. I didn't know it was General Cromwell. They were discussing marriage terms.'

'It must be a Cromwell son or daughter then,' Betty said.

'The gentleman with him seemed to be driving a hard bargain,' the eaves-dropper went on. 'General Cromwell meeting his match I guess.'

Ann, picking up the gossip from the margins of the group, said, 'It's all conjecture.'

'No smoke without fire,' Betty retorted. 'We've yet to see what becomes of that Charity consorting with Thomas Mannory's cart lad Hal.'

'That Charity!' The eavesdropper had more to tell. 'The other morning she was in the Inn courtyard with a man I've never seen before. He looked to be all over her, clasping her hands. I thought he would embrace her any minute.'

Ann could not resist outfacing them all. 'It's Thomas has an interest in Charity,' she said. 'He rescued her when a soldier raped her.'

The effect was all that she hoped for and more. Attention had left her mother and questions rained on her. But a pang of guilt restrained her sense of power, and she refused to elaborate. James called her, and she gladly went off with him.

But all was not well with James.

Over the winter months James had multiplied the curing and marketing of rabbit skins. As Ann had discovered, rabbit proved a less expensive alternative to beef or mutton, and was no less tasty. She learnt to cook it well, sometimes mixed with bacon for added flavour, although boiled bacon continued as a staple.

Her reports of rabbit for sale in the weekly market prompted James to seek out warreners, in the forest, in the park, talking with them when they brought their trapped and paunched rabbits in to market. He became their chief buyer, for there seemed to be no limit to the quantity of rabbit skins that Kiffin could arrange to export.

Compared with the tanning of big heavy cow hides, curing rabbit and other fine skins in a salt and alum solution took only a few weeks. Then they needed to be washed and gently dried, worked by hand over wooden bars to soften the fibres and finally to have a mixture of oil and egg white rubbed into them.

His father Jacob Mannory watched these developments, noting the time and space being taken up by the fine hides. Some of his tanning pits were now permanently occupied with the process, and the alum which Thomas brought from the brewers in Southwark had to be stored somewhere.

That lad, whom James had beaten so soundly a year ago, seemed to have acquired the knack of cutting and pulling the fine membrane off the underside of skins. Yet a special skill such as that one was surely not all that his parents had in mind when they had arranged his apprenticeship as a tanner.

'Apprentice Mark,' he said to James one lunch hour when there was a break in toil. They had gone up to the office to resolve some accounting queries. 'That lad,' he said, 'spends a great deal of his time on your fine hides.'

'I was relieved to find something at which he could excel,' James said. 'He's interested in the elements we use in the curing, too. Quite inventive in a quiet way.'

'These elements, as you call them, besides the curing, take up more and more of the yard. What are your intentions?'

'Why, to build up the trade. The market is there, the transport, and it's already profitable. For you as well as for me.'

'On this scale, it is interfering with tanning, competing for space.' Jacob voiced a decision. 'I'll soon require you to find another yard.'

'What, relinquish my position here? Go somewhere else? And where, among the tanners in this town, would there be one that could allow me space, any more than you want to do?'

'That is your choice,' Jacob said. 'I'll not set a time limit, but I am unlikely to change my mind on this matter.'

James went down the steep stairs in a daze. The months of developing this new trade had been exhilarating. He had not, he felt, neglected his duties as yard foreman. Acquiring and instructing the newer skills had been satisfying. He had not thought about how his father might view the impact on the Tanyard. His Tanyard.

They were taking their meal at midday again now that days were lengthening. He walked home with worries cascading round in his head.

There was nothing on the table, no smell of cooking. 'Ann?' he called. A faint cry responded from the bedroom. He bounded up the stairs, angry.

Ann was only half dressed, propped up on the bed.

'Where's the meal?' he shouted.

'Don't hit me!' Ann cried. 'Please don't hit me! I did try. I feel so ill.'

He registered then the smell of vomit and the earthenware chamber pot on the floor.

'What ails you?' he said surlily.

'I think,' Ann was hesitant. 'I think I may be with child.'

With his foot James slid the chamber pot across the floorboards as far as possible. Then he sat down on the bed, and looked uncomprehending at his wife. Ill, because with child. Would this sickness continue all nine months until the birth? And he newly confronted with Jacob's pronouncement.

'My father wants me out of his Tanyard,' was all he could think to say. 'How are we to live through this coming year?'

Ann swung her legs off the bed. 'It's better in the afternoon,' she said. 'I did manage until today, but it was worse this morning. I'll come down and find some food for you.'

'A hunk of bread?' James tone was bitter.

'It's not just the smell of cooking,' Ann said as he ate. 'My stomach refuses food. I could hardly face the meals I've cooked for you the last week.'

'If this is going to get any worse, we'd be better off employing a cook.'

'Charity is a good cook,' Ann said. 'We could ask her. She used to be a friend, but I haven't seen her to talk to for months.'

'I'd rather that than eat in the Tanyard again,' James said.

He did not take immediate action. But he could see that Ann was truthful about her condition, and he needed his meals. So one Tuesday evening he walked up to West Street and the Attfields' house.

When his sister opened the door he was surprised to see who was there; not just Ralph and Abigail and their little son, but Charity and Hal and Thomas as well, and a man who somehow looked familiar. The silence, and the small Bible open on Ralph's knee, suggested that he was intruding.

'Come in and welcome!' Abigail said. Ralph closed the Bible and stood up. 'We've started meeting on a Tuesday evening,' he said, 'Just to read and pray together. We were about to conclude.'

The stranger nodded to Ralph who opened the door for him to leave. James sat down. Abigail picked up a sleepy Simon and held him on her lap. 'This is a rare visit,' she said. 'We're glad to see you.'

'I've actually come to ask a favour.' James said. 'My wife Ann is with child, and sick every morning, sometimes even through the day. She can scarcely prepare meals. What I came to ask is whether you could spare Charity, perhaps a few days a week, to prepare and cook a meal for us. Ann would be very grateful.'

He did not notice Charity's sharp intake of breath, but

201

Abigail did. She was aware of how the walks with Simon had changed direction, aware too of her haste when buying bread. She looked at Charity and caught the alarm in her face. 'May we discuss it, James?' she said. 'We'll give you an answer in a day or two.'

'Before you go,' Thomas said, 'I've got some pamphlets I was going to bring you from London. You'll have heard about the Royalist risings?'

'Newsbooks?' James said.

'I did bring a newsbook, and had a peep into it – Scots about to invade, and castles held for the King. No, these are Leveller leaflets.'

James held out his hand.

Thomas gave him a package, saying, 'As the Army is off fighting again, the Levellers are taking other means to promote their cause. John Lilburne sent word to ask you to distribute these among people in Farnham who may support them.'

'Distribute? I…'

'I'm just the messenger,' Thomas said.

There seemed to be nothing more to be said, so James took his leave and left.

'Charity dear,' Abigail said as the door closed behind him. 'Would you care to tell us what is troubling you?'

Charity looked down, saying nothing. Not long ago she would have fled upstairs, but there was an accepting warmth about this family. The others waited silently. Finally Hal said, 'Is it that rumour?'

'In a way,' Charity said. She took a deep breath, and at last began to speak. 'I told Ann what had befallen me. Because she needed comfort. And now she seems to be telling everyone.'

'The rumour involves me as well,' Thomas said, 'that fighting that soldier was for my own ends, and bringing you here too. I've been struggling over what Ann said, what she has been spreading.'

Charity looked at him, whom Abigail had called a good man.

'Struggling to forgive,' he said.

'Why should you forgive something so mean? A hurt?' Hal said.

Thomas did not reply at once. Then he said, 'We've prayed often in church, sort of by rote, "Forgive us our trespasses, as we forgive those who trespass against us." I'd never thought much about it, until we read it together in almost our first meeting.'

'Forgive the inexcusable?' Hal said.

'I suppose it's like refusing to hold against someone the hurt they have done,' Abigail said. 'A sort of letting go.'

'That doesn't change what has happened,' Charity said.

'In a roundabout way,' Ralph said, 'it seems that forgiving changes things for the person doing the forgiving. It says,' he flipped through pages to find the place, 'that our being forgiven somehow depends on us forgiving.'

'I thought I had forgiven Ann, but it keeps coming into my mind,' Thomas said.

'I expect it's a process,' Ralph said. 'Going on letting go.'

Charity looked round the extended family, this family that she was beginning to trust. 'So,' she said, 'do I have to go and cook for Ann?'

'You don't have to,' Abigail said. 'There's no obligation. You can choose. A free choice.'

Sleep eluded Charity in the little bedroom that had become her own. It was Abigail James had asked about her cooking for Ann. She, like him, had assumed the decision rested with Abigail. But Abigail insisted that it was her choice. She, Charity, had to choose. It was her choice whether to agree to cook, or to refuse.

Tossing and turning, she thought around this matter of choice. Choices about her had generally been made by other people. She had not chosen to become part of the Attfield household. When back then she had first arrived she had also lain awake, sent away by her Grandmother's choice, handed over to Abigail by Thomas' choice. She wondered then if Thomas had chosen, or simply obeyed Grandmother. But he must have chosen to come to the farm.

That time when she and Ann had crouched over the new-lit fire and she had told Ann her story - it had just happened, it had not been a deliberate choice. She had not considered whether Ann would spread the story. Had she known, would she have chosen otherwise ?

And now it was she who had to choose, to decide. She did not like the idea of being subject to Ann, being controlled by her. And she feared her tongue, feared being exposed by her to people's curiosity.

These rambling thoughts brought her no nearer to a decision, nor to sleep. Somehow, she thought, I need to be taken by surprise.

Her first surprise had nothing to do with Ann.

Yet another showery day and Simon was under everyone's feet. 'I'll take him out, rain or no rain,' Charity said, 'even if it is only along the road.' They had not gone far when Walter

Hutchcroft caught up with them. So engrossed had she been in her own thoughts the evening before that she had scarcely noticed that he was there. He must have met Ralph in the street and both slipped in almost un-noticed, and he had left as discretely.

'I've spent the night in the Inn,' he said, falling into step beside her. 'I have to press on to Southampton, but what joy to have crossed your path! A chance to get to know each other better. Where can we go out of the rain?'

They went down to the church and sat in one of the few seats inside, where Walter started to talk about Martha.

'She had such a lively spirit,' he said. 'She loved to hear about new things. She was eager to learn all she could about the New World. No end to her ideas of what we could do or make if we went there. And when John Woodbridge invited me to go with him to Massachusetts, her excitement knew no bounds.'

Charity smiled. 'I suppose that is what my grandmother meant when she said that she had her nose into everything. But from her it was a criticism. Or (a new thought) was she trying to warn me?'

'Are you like Martha in character as well as in looks, then?'

'As a child I was like that. But after what happened, I shut away, kept to what seemed safe, just the people I knew.'

He did not rush into a reply. Then quietly he said, 'Can you tell me what happened?'

'I've only ever talked about it once. It didn't occur to me that afterwards it would be gossiped around the town.'

'But I am your father,' he said gently. 'I would guard your privacy.'

Was this the same man who, on their previous meeting, had been all excitement? She looked across the wide church, wondering about the risk of trusting him, of trusting anyone. He did not press her, but sat silently waiting.

What did it mean to have a father, the father whom, as a young man, grandmother had decried?

She gave herself a little shake and turned to him. She could not postpone this choice, the choice between trusting him or retreating.

She started to tell him about that night, about the soldier, the rape, the rescue; about her own sense of guilt, of shame. Telling a second time was easier than the first had been, and being here in this ancient church was somehow reassuring. Walter heard her out without interrupting or prompting. As she lapsed into silence he said, 'So I owe your life to Thomas.'

Then he said, 'Maybe what your grandmother told you about me and about your mother was to try to protect you. She was appalled when I got Martha with child. We were young and passionate and heedless. Maybe she feared that you would repeat the pattern.'

'If relations with a man are like what it was with that soldier, I most certainly would not.' Charity was emphatic.

'It doesn't need to be,' Walter said. 'For Martha and me it was pure pleasure. And you, dear Charity, are the beautiful result.'

He looked round the church then, as if for the first time. 'This should be a place of healing,' he said. 'God of mercy, be pleased to heal Charity's wounded spirit. Free her.'

'Do you think he can?' Charity said.

'I believe he has already started,' Walter said. 'I'm no theologian, but I do believe.'

As if sensing a conclusion Simon, who had been investigating every corner of the church, came over to them and put his hands in Charity's own.

'Oh Simon! You're so cold! Let's go and run in the churchyard and warm you up.'

With Walter it was more than running. He dodged between tombstones, hid behind a big sarcophagus, sprang out to Simon's squealed delight. Charity joined in with abandon until all three ended in a breathless bundle of laughter.

'Now I must hasten to Southampton,' Walter said, catching his breath. 'John fears that negotiating with the King is going to be a long and wearisome business. So he has called for his wife and children to join him in England. He is busy in town, and I am off to make final sailing arrangements on his behalf.'

They parted on the Attfields' doorstep.

Chapter 16 - Choices

Choices were being made all over the country, choices made and then sometimes reversed, loyalties switched.

Back in February, when the governor of Pembroke Castle was ordered to hand over to his designated successor, he refused to obey until pay was sent for his garrison troops. Instead of paying, Parliament declared him and his troops to be traitors unless they surrendered the Castle. He took only three weeks, weeks perhaps full of weighing up choices, to declare for the King. With a fellow sympathiser he mustered several thousand men.

General Fairfax sent Cromwell west to put down this royalist rebellion.

In Ireland, the Parliamentary General switched sides, linking up with his erstwhile Irish enemies along with the Scots, although rivalries in Scotland made them unreliable allies. The House of Commons kept passing motions in favour of negotiations with the King and then overturning them as events unfolded.

Just before Easter Lydia's playmate Ben Hewling was spending a few days in the Kiffin home.

'Shall you be an apprentice when you are older?' Lydia asked him.

'I suppose so,' Ben said. 'Why do you ask?'

'Apprentices riot in the streets. And some of them get killed.'

'My father says they are supporting the King,' Ben said.

'But some are not, he says. It's hard to know what's right.'

They arranged the Backgammon board and started to play, until they heard William come into the house.

'You're soon home,' Hanna said.

'Rioters are out again, a big crowd,' he said. 'They've taken the City gates at Ludgate and Newgate. It's said the Lord Mayor has fled to the Tower. Much good may that do him.'

'Father! Mother! Look!' Lydia was at the window. 'Look! Soldiers!'

'Come away children,' Hanna said.

'No, look! They're marching through Moorgate, lots of them.'

'They're Militiamen,' William said, 'Meant to guard the City. They keep being called in, to quell riots and scatter crowds.'

'I hope no one gets hurt this time,' Hanna said.

The pretext for such demonstrations was usually a legitimate petition, but with such large crowds gathering in support, they could easily turn into a riot. Today the troops managed to disperse the crowd without hurt, and arrested some of the apparent leaders. Other riots had worse outcomes, as when a County magazine seized by rioters accidentally blew up, killing a hundred people.

'Shall we be governed by rioters?' Hanna said. Piecemeal, war had broken out all over again. But it was threats to shipping which most concerned William.

Warships of the Navy were anchored in the Downs, the broad bay between the Thames and Dover. Sheltered from all but the most severe gales, it was an anchorage for many ships besides the warships - merchantmen waiting for favourable wind and tide to take them south into the English Channel, or across the Baltic Sea, or round into the Thames estuary and thence to shipyards in London.

The seamen there, with only maintenance to keep them occupied, were an easy prey for Royalist propaganda, much as the Army had been for the Levellers. Indeed, as if taking their cue from the Leveller methods, Royalists distributed leaflets to every ship in the Fleet.

Vice-Admiral Batten was in command, a Presbyterian and life-long seafarer with an eye to the main chance. When the excluded Members of Parliament, including Waller, Massie and Poynz, had fled in a small ship across to Calais, Batten at first intercepted them and brought their vessel back to the Downs. But following a council of war on board his ship, he allowed them to proceed to the Netherlands.

So, suspicious that Batten might be colluding with his sailors' royalist sympathies, Parliament (now dominated by Independents) dismissed him from command.

'Do you remember, when James Mannory was staying with us,' William said to Hanna, 'he and I visited John Lilburne in the Tower, and met Colonel Rainsborough?'

'Yes, I remember,' Hanna said. 'Hadn't Rainsborough been attending Army debates in Putney?'

'He had, and giving rational support to the idea of votes for all, and even a republic. He's been put in command of the Fleet.'

'I thought he already was,' Hanna said.

'He was. Then Parliament became afraid that he would spread Leveller ideas in the Fleet and rescinded the appointment. Now he is back as Admiral. They can't deny his ability.'

It did not last. The sailors took control. They forcibly prevented Rainsborough from entering his flagship, and declared for the King. On land they linked with Kentish royalists, secured several castles and besieged Dover. They then sent to the Admiralty Commissioners, justifying their actions and calling for a personal treaty with the King and an end to the Army.

Meanwhile shipyards all the way up the Thames were disputed over.

News travelled fast.

'The Earl of Warwick is replacing Rainsborough,' William reported. 'He was Lord High Admiral before the New Model Army was formed.'

'I remember meeting him,' Hanna said. 'The kind of man whom men respect.'

'The sailors love him,' William said. 'He's made sure the warship squadron in Portsmouth keeps loyal to Parliament, but he hasn't managed to get the seamen in the Downs to change their minds. And that slippery customer Batten went to Portsmouth, and came away with a ship in support of the King.'

A couple of weeks later the mutineers from the Downs sailed their nine warships across to the neutral Netherlands and to the sheltered inlet of Helvoetsluis.

'Young Prince Charles,' William said, 'will have hastened there from his exile in France.'

'He's young isn't he, only eighteen or so?' Hanna said.

'Raised in royal courts,' William said. 'I doubt he knows much about ships and naval warfare. But as Prince of Wales he'll be expecting to take command of this little royalist fleet.'

'So now it's war at sea as well as on land,' Hanna said. 'What will happen to your trade?

A week or so after James' request, weeks in which Charity had avoided thinking about the choice she had to make, the day dawned bright and warm, too bright, probably, to last. In this cold wet summer it came as an invitation to go out. 'Shall we go for a walk?' she asked Simon.

'Walk!' he beamed. Then as she fastened his shoes he announced, 'Meadow!'

They slipped through past the church and the rectory to the green expanse of the meadow. Hawthorn bushes were a shower of white blossom. Cow parsley waved its white crowns, and the meadow grass was aglow with golden dandelions and hawkweed. Charity stood still to breathe in the warm scent of the hawthorn, while Simon ran in purposeless circles, just for the joy of wet grass and space and sunshine.

Although it was still very early, soon she felt they should be returning to the house. Suddenly, dark clouds built up, obscuring the sun.

'Come Simon!' she said. 'It's going to rain.'

They ran as fast as his little legs would go, up past the Rectory and then, rounding the corner into Church Lane, it was as if great buckets of water were being emptied from the sky. Charity hammered on the door of the first house they came to. And James opened it.

'Please may we shelter?' Charity panted.

James drew them inside.

'You're very early,' he said. 'Did you come to see my wife?'

'We actually went for a walk in the meadow,' Charity said,

'when the shower came. And yes please, may I see Ann?'

'I'll see,' James said. Funny, Charity thought watching this middling height stout man climbing the stair; funny, he's not at all like his brother Thomas to look at. Thomas is tall and lean, and quite handsome in a way, not unlike Abigail.

'She'll be down in a moment,' James said. 'Mornings are difficult for her. I must to the Tanyard,' and he left.

Sitting there, trying to shake the rain off cap and garments, Charity suddenly giggled. Taken by surprise indeed! Whatever was she to say to Ann?

Ann was neatly dressed when she came down the stair. 'Well,' she said, 'I haven't seen you for a long time. Did James ask you about cooking for us?'

'He did, and that's why I've come,' Charity said. 'Please could you tell me what you are asking me to do?'

'Oh, just prepare some meals,' Ann said. 'It was James' idea. Not necessarily every day. I'll pay you of course, as I did for the embroidery you did for me.'

'Who would purchase the ingredients?' Charity asked, ignoring the servant implication. 'And would you want me to cook the meal here, or to do it at home and bring it to you once it was cooked?'

'I hadn't thought,' Ann said, 'though I do find the smell of cooking nauseating.'

'I could do a big stew, and then you could heat up what you needed as you liked,' Charity said.

'Will you always be bringing the child?' Ann said, as if it were already settled. She looked with distaste at Simon again trying to dismember a faggot.

'Not if I'm carrying a cauldron!' Charity laughed. 'But Ann,

I'll need to ask Abigail anyway. I'll take Simon home how, and tell you later what we decide.'

The shower had eased, the encounter had avoided any personal topic, and hastening up the hill Charity had a small feeling of achievement.

Thus it began. Abigail showed Charity how to keep account of what she spent on Ann's behalf, heartened to find that not only could Charity read but she responded well to figures and recording them. Together they doubled the quantity they normally cooked, and Charity staggered down the hill to deliver the pan on Tuesdays and Fridays. Once or twice Hal happened by, and carried it for her.

As the weeks passed Ann no longer suffered from nausea, but she did not attempt to end the arrangement. Now that she knew for certain that she was with child she spent ever more time with her sister-in-law Joan and Joan's baby daughter. There too she kept up with the town gossip in which her mother was the expert.

Charity had delivered the latest stew to the empty house and was about to return home with the cleaned-out pot from the previous week. As she opened the door, Thomas came along the cobbles.

'Is anyone at home?' he asked.

'No,' Charity said. 'I've just brought them their meal – I cook for them a couple of days a week.'

'Do you now!' Thomas said. 'Can you let me in for a minute? I've brought some newsbooks and stuff for James.' He piled them neatly on a shelf beside the chimney breast. 'So you're cooking for them, and cooking for Abigail, and caring for Simon – what a lass you're proving to be!'

'I just help Abigail,' Charity said.

Thomas stood looking at her curiously. 'For a long time,' he said hesitantly, 'I thought of you as a victim. And I didn't know how to relate to a victim.'

Charity smiled at him. 'Maybe that's how I've thought of myself. Other people deciding what's to be done with me.'

Thomas chuckled. 'I can tell you now, I didn't at all know what to do with you when I brought you to Farnham. Both of us obeying your grandmother, and I had no proper plan. Thank God for Abigail.'

'I can echo that,' Charity said. She looked at him thoughtfully. 'I suppose we need to adjust how we see another person as we get to know each other.'

Standing here in someone else's kitchen seemed an odd context for such a conversation. Here she had put Ann in her confidence. Here surely Thomas had been embarrassed. Yet she wanted to clarify to him how she had felt.

'When you left me with Abigail and then disappeared,' she said, 'I felt you had betrayed me. But you are saying it was just that you didn't know how to relate to me as a victim.'

He nodded.

'I didn't know how to relate either,' Charity said. 'I'd remembered you as my hero, my deliverer, but after you came back to the farm I didn't know who or what you were.'

'A very ordinary man,' Thomas said, 'A humdrum carter.'

'Humdrum? Thoughtful I'd say. And I have you to thank for bringing my father here.'

They faced each other silently for a long moment. Then Thomas turned towards the door saying, 'Back to work' and they left the house, he one way towards his stable by the long bridge, she uphill towards West Street and home, but not before Ann, returning from visiting her family, had seen him go.

'I've delivered the stew,' Charity told her, 'and Thomas brought some pamphlets for James.'

Chapter 17 - Change

A day did not pass without William conferring with fellow merchants and ship owners, and in mid June he brought home a chart. He spread it on their dining table, and he and Hanna examined it together.

'So here is Helvoetsluis, wretched name to get your tongue round. Not far from Antwerp in the Netherlands. Up a wide inlet, a perfect refuge.'

'And that's where the mutineers have taken the men-o'-war?' Hanna said.

'They have. Nine or ten of them. A ready-made fleet at the service of Prince Charles! And look, those warships are only a few days' sailing from Amsterdam and our trading base.'

He ran his finger over the chart. 'They're within reach of English ports too, and the seamen turned royalist are familiar with the way, the hazards of the Goodwin Sands.'

'Before this, the fighting was all on land, wasn't it?' Hanna said.

'Well, now it's both on land and at sea it seems. You remember there were royalist riots in Essex?' William pointed to the coast north of the Thames. 'They took over Colchester, up a river running from the coast. General Fairfax is besieging the town.'

'I read about it in the newsbooks,' Hanna said.

'The latest is that three ships sailed from Helvoetsluis and tried to take supplies up the river. A local garrison drove them back.'

'Oh Will, we thought the war was over, and now it's worse

than ever. Right on our doorstep.' Hanna leant over the chart. 'From Helvoetsluis they could block your Baltic trade.'

'It'll be a matter of cat and mouse,' William said. 'They could cross over and attack anywhere along our coast.'

A month later, at the end of July, Prince Charles did just that. He sent his fleet beyond Colchester, but local magistrates with a few troops prevented them from making a landing. So the next day the fleet sailed south to the Downs, and started seizing merchant ships.

'He'll send them to capture more prizes,' William said. 'In conditions like this, you can't rely on the loyalty of ships' captains. Merchantmen turned pirates.'

Hanna got out the chart again and traced her finger over the coastlines. 'If his ships stay in the Downs, they can easily sail out and attack,' she said. 'What will become of our trade with Amsterdam?'

'I suppose with a fair wind our ships could slip across from the Thames to Amsterdam,' Williams said, 'but I'd not want to risk them passing the Downs. And it'll be a brave merchant-man who risks the narrow straights of Dover to head into the English Channel.'

'Didn't you say the warships at Portsmouth are loyal to Parliament?' Hanna said. 'Can't they protect shipping in the Channel?'

'If they remain in Portsmouth,' Williams said. 'Merchant ships coming from the west will do better not to rely on them, but go up Southampton Water. That is safe enough.'

He looked at the chart again, at the Isle of Wight like a barrier protecting Southampton.

'So much depends on wind and weather, and this summer

has been foul,' William said. 'One way or another we have to change the way we operate until there is peace.'

The weather was foul indeed.

When Thomas went to collect his cartage pay, Piggott hesitated from counting out the coins. 'Sit down a moment,' he said.

Surprised, Thomas sat, and waited.

'Another bad summer,' Piggott said. 'Cold and wet.'

Surely, Thomas thought, he's not sat me down just to talk about the weather.

'Poor harvest last year, and the same now,' Piggott said.

'Is grain short?' Thomas asked.

'That's it!' The question released Piggott to talk. 'Not much coming in from hereabouts. Little to spare for London.'

Is he trying to tell me, Thomas thought, that there'll be nothing for me to take to the City? Is he trying to end the contract? Instead he said 'What's London doing for grain?'

'They're importing from Holland, the Netherlands.'

'Didn't Holland have bad weather too?' Thomas said.

'Ah, yes. But they have big grain stores, built up in good years. Clever, those Dutchmen. Profitable for them.' The touch of bitterness switched then. 'Now the Royalists have ships, it's even risky carrying from Holland.'

'Are you saying there'll be no grain for me to carry to London?'

Piggott looked Thomas in the eyes. 'I've no complaint about your services,' he said. 'The situation is uncertain. They've started bringing grain in from France, to Southampton.'

'I could carry it from there, if you'd like,' Thomas said.

'Store it in your granary or mine till you know the demand for London.'

Slowly Piggott sat back in his chair as he absorbed Thomas' suggestion. 'You could carry it straight on to London,' he said.

'Well, no,' Thomas said, surprising himself. 'Southampton and back with loading time would take three days at least, enough out of each week. A local carter would have to take it onwards as required.'

'He'd not need to go all the way to the City,' Piggott said. 'I've been negotiating transferring cargo to Thames barges at Teddington. Bigger capacity than carts.'

Thomas sat silently as Piggott ruminated, almost looking through Thomas.

'Very well,' he said at last. 'With your agreement, I'll make a new contract and you can fetch grain from Southampton as it becomes available. No doubt you'll find plenty else to carry both ways.' He stood up and held out his hand. 'Agreed?' he said.

A few days later Thomas happened to meet James. 'By the way,' he said, 'From now on I'll not be going to London, so I won't be able to bring you newsbooks and stuff from the City.'

'What about skins to Kiffin?'

'Oh yes, those. Piggott is arranging for the cargo to go on by barge, so I'll be carrying only as far as Teddington. You'll have to find out the loading arrangements and check with the barge masters.'

On almost Thomas' last trip to the City, John Woodbridge made a point of meeting him while he lodged with the Kiffins.

'I have decided to move down to Southampton to be at hand when we are needed to negotiate with His Majesty,' he said. 'Would you be prepared to carry our baggage down there for us?'

'I could take you as well,' Thomas laughed, 'if you could put up with the discomfort of travelling in my cart.'

James went home early and sat down to think. Ann was out. The only sound was the crooning of hens in their little pen. At least they were profitable. Sometime they even laid enough eggs for some to be sold in the market. He sat down and wished his thoughts could offer a solution to his mounting pile of worry.

Surprised to find him at home, Ann said, 'James! Are you ill?'

'No,' James said. 'A lot on my mind.'

'It's a cold meal today,' Ann said. 'I'll slice the bacon and bread and things, and then we can talk.'

Not something we do, James thought. Not constructive talk. Not airing our worries and seeking answers. But maybe Ann has no worries? About the babe? About me? She might not realise that I do have worries. All this went round in his head, before he had had a bite to eat, and some of it new to his mind.

They ate in silence, bread and bacon and a relish of some sort, and ale as usual. 'Ann,' he said at last. 'There are some things I need to tell you.'

'About me?' Ann said, alarmed.

'About us, about the situation we are in.'

'I didn't know we were in any sort of situation,' Ann said.

'That's why I need to tell you,' James said. 'First, about the Tanyard. My father has told me I must find my own premises, because he says the fine hide work is taking up too much space and time. I think he is mistaken, but the Tanyard is his and he controls what happens there.'

'What premises, where?' Ann said.

'There are none that I can find,' James said. 'Then, Thomas is no longer to go to London, and if the skins are to be delivered there I have to set up some other means. Money may be short as a result.' He took a deep breath. 'We must stop employing Charity to cook.'

'Oh, what a shame!' Ann said.

'But you're well now, aren't you,' James said. 'There is no reason now why you should not cook, and you have little else to do.'

'I'm sewing for the babe,' Ann said.

'Come come, that cannot take all your time.'

Ann looked round the tidy little room, tidy except for a pile of pamphlets which had lain on a shelf for too long. 'What about those pamphlets?' she said, inconsequentially, 'Those Thomas brought for you to distribute.'

James reached them down and looked at them. Leveller protests and demands, much as before in a different form. 'Lilburne shouldn't have sent them,' he said, with initial indignation. Then he said, 'Oh Ann, I can't go round Farnham handing out these pamphlets. People here don't work in this way. Whatever would they think of me, promoting Leveller designs?'

'But you're always so interested in the newsbooks and pamphlets you read,' Ann said. 'You talk of justice and all that...'

'It's like you once said,' James said flatly. 'Theory, news, and I do nothing about it. Except fighting briefly, and that achieved nothing. Look at the way we are now, with war going on all over again. Lilburne and others working away in London, petitioning Parliament and so on, and yet nothing seems to change as a result.'

Ann looked at him silently, trying to process what she had heard.

'I'm sorry,' she said at last, 'I didn't know.'

'And now this babe,' James said.

'A baby doesn't have to be expensive,' Ann said. 'My mother, and Joan too, are longing to hand things on to me, though up to now they say I have been too proud to accept them.'

'I didn't want a babe, I just wanted to enjoy you,' James said, 'and I haven't been much good at that either.'

'James!' Ann exclaimed. She put her arms round him, and he pulled her onto his lap. 'We'll have to get through somehow,' she said.

'You'll not tell anyone what I've told you, will you,' James said.

Ann said nothing, but her eyes spoke.

'Promise me Ann. This isn't a topic for title tattle round the town. Promise me you won't talk about it.'

With difficulty, Ann promised.

Thomas had never seen the sea before, though they told him that Southampton Water was not exactly the sea but only led into it. The long estuary certainly held many ships, anchored or coming or going. He began to familiarise himself with the surroundings, the loading quays, the warehouses, stabling and where to sleep if necessary. He learnt of the double tides which swept round the Isle of Wight from two directions, tides which could benefit ships waiting to enter the estuary. He also learnt by experience that though tides were predictable, winds were not. Contrary winds or no wind at all could delay ships' arrival, delay his loading.

The goods he brought down from Farnham had been transferred to the bonded warehouse with all the paperwork completed, and still the right ship had not arrived. Sitting in one of the alehouses, trying to avoid spending out on too many tankards of ale, he was joined by a smartly dressed young man.

'I should have been back on the Island by now,' he said. Seeing Thomas' puzzled look he added 'Isle of Wight, short way across the Solent sea,' gesturing vaguely. 'Came here to collect and despatch letters.' He patted a satchel held close over his shoulder although he was sitting down. 'Important,' he said. 'Have to keep them with me.'

'Isle of Wight,' Thomas said. 'Isn't that where the King is?'

'Carisbrook Castle, Colonel Hammond's guest, actually a prisoner. Guards posted round about.'

'Are you one of them?' Thomas asked.

'Me? No!' He extended his hand. 'Frank's the name. Colonel's staff, travelled with him all over the country, all the battles, looked after him. He's Governor of the Isle of Wight now. Thankless task he has. Quite friendly with His Majesty, at first that is, and his Reverend Uncle was an out and out royalist. Had to leave the Island.'

Frank took a long draft of his ale. 'There's others who have been told to leave. Too clever and plotting all the time.' He looked out of the window as the dusk thickened. 'Another dark night. Escapes get planned for dark nights.'

'But I suppose the guards prevent it,' Thomas said.

'The first one back in April, the King had a long cord, and his accomplice got himself out of the barred window, but his

Majesty got stuck. Belly too big! The guards, they wouldn't have been any use, too much wine, but of course we got him back in.'

'A bit embarrassing for him!' Thomas said.

'Reckons himself divinely appointed, so he can do no wrong.' He laughed. 'We foiled another escape attempt a couple of weeks ago. Keeps everyone on their toes. The King doesn't like all this guarding. Has words with Colonel Hammond at times.'

One of the Harbour Master's staff whom Thomas had talked with, came over to them. 'The tugs are bringing in some of the ships on the swell tide,' he said. 'They've rowed down on the ebb to be ready. The wind's died right down.'

'I'll be off first thing then,' Frank said, 'so long as it doesn't blow up again.'

The sacks of grain had to be unloaded, checked, and loaded onto the wagons waiting alongside Thomas'. The process swallowed up the morning, so that despite the long August day the convoy made it only a short way past Winchester by evening, and the best of another day to reach Farnham. Piggott came to check the consignment before it was secured for the night. Thomas sorted the rest of his load for distribution, and tended the horses with Hal's help.

'By the time I've done the Teddington run, I'll not be home before the week is out,' he said. 'Judging by the order book, you and the small cart are barely keeping up. We're going to need another cart.'

'And another carter,' Hal said. 'Are you coming to the conventicle?'

'Is today Tuesday?' Thomas said. 'I've lost track of time.'

Late as it was, he went, if only to catch a glimpse of Charity.

'It's not comfortable,' Thomas said, reviewing the makeshift seats he had contrived in his cart.

John Woodbridge laughed. 'You should have seen us when we moved to Andover from Massachusetts Bay. Two days over rough country, with carts loaded with all our furniture and goods.'

'Baggage too,' Walter said, 'and the children.'

'The older children walked,' John said, 'but when they tired they needed to go on one of the carts. We're not unused to discomfort.'

'It was worth the effort,' John said as they set off, continuing the conversation they had begun while loading Thomas' cart at Teddington. 'Andover is a pleasant settlement.'

'The Merrimack river is not far off, and Andover has a good supply of sweet water,' Walter said. 'The Indians had cleared some of the forest before smallpox killed them off, so there were clearings ready to be settled.'

'What sort of country is it?' Thomas asked.

'A few mountains, undulating by the rivers, and more fertile than where we'd been on the coast.'

'A lot of fruit grows wild,' Walter said. 'We found strawberries, raspberries, plums, blueberries, there for the picking. We've learnt how to use the Indian corn. We call it maize.'

'And there is game in the forest,' John said.

They jogged on through towns and villages, stopping occasionally where Thomas had goods to deliver. Coming through the heather and gorse wilderness of Bagshot heath, Walter looked with distaste at this contrast to familiar Wiltshire downland and Massachusetts river valleys. He asked Thomas 'Have you ever thought of emigrating?'

'I can't say I have,' Thomas said.

'Your little conventicle might be in trouble some day,' John said.

'If it comes to that,' Thomas said, 'we'll have to weather it. I get the impression from the letters in the Bible that the writers have plenty of advice for the persecuted.'

John Woodbridge smiled. 'You're contented with your life as it is?'

Thomas nodded. He had begun to realise that even he had some ambition akin to that of James. 'I enjoy building up this business, and making the acquaintance of different people.'

They were nearing Farnham now. 'I shall soon return to the New World,' Walter said, 'to take care of John's property there. I'd like to take Charity with me, find her a husband – and a wife for myself – establish a family in Andover. She is, after all, already my family, my daughter.'

Take her away? Thomas thought. Is that what she would choose?

Walter was still talking, getting into his stride. 'Her mother, my Martha, had a really adventurous spirit. If Charity is truly like her, she would make an ideal colonist. I have a feeling that such a spirit may be locked inside her, about to burst into flower.'

John Woodbridge smiled at him. 'You had better ask her while we are in Farnham this night,' he said.

Thomas went home to the Tanyard, finding himself dejected. His passengers went to the Bush Inn. Setting out to Winchester the next morning, all he wanted was to ask whether

Walter had seen Charity, but instead he said nothing. The day was chill and misty. The wheat fields they passed were lodged and flattened by rain storms, some damply rotting.

Eventually he blurted out, 'What did she say?'

Precarious though their seat was, John Woodbridge had fallen asleep, and Walter dozed. 'Who?' he said, jerking awake.

Thomas was obliged to repeat his question. 'Charity, what did she say?'

'About the New World?' Walter said. 'She said little. It would be a big decision, a big choice, for her. I do not know what she will choose.'

Chapter 18 - Abe Trussler

Ann had not realised how hard it would be to keep her promise to James. Yet seeing him distressed and vulnerable, their roles somehow reversed, she found that she did want to keep it. As compensation there were other topics for gossip, with a small garrison now in the Castle, and speculation about Charity and her possible swains.

'Thomas and she were alone in my house,' she said. 'What might they have got up to?' And her mother would chip in about the strange man she had been seen with, and Hal. But as time went on, gossip began to lose its flavour for Ann, with too little to talk about, until an event which was the talk of the town. Abe Trussler was discovered, several days dead, in his own ramshackle house.

'He's got his deserts at last,' was a sentiment not uncommon among the gossips.

'That woman who cooked for him, where was she?' one woman said to Betty Gary.

'Which woman?' Betty said. 'None stayed long with him, ill-tempered man.'

'Odd that none of his workers suspected anything,' another said, 'though they do say he often left them to it.'

'Only to rush out in a temper. I know. My husband has worked for him for years, can't think why.'

'You would have thought… and they began to construct

blame, blame of people who failed to know he was dead, blame of the deceased himself.

Hal, intent on business, was perhaps the last person to hear of Abe's death.

'Did you hear that Abe Trussler has died?' he said as he and Thomas went through their evening ritual of tending the horses.

'Two days before anyone realised,' Thomas said. 'That tells you what a bad lot he was.'

'He had a cough all last year, which got worse,' Hal said. 'And no family.'

'He had nothing to commend him,' Thomas said.

'He was a person,' Hal said.

Thomas stopped what he was doing and looked searchingly at Hal. 'I told you to have nothing to do with him.'

'Well. Yes,' Hal mumbled. 'But I did feel sorry for him.'

He was relieved that Thomas did not question him further.

Niblett the attorney quickly arranged the interment. Hal stood alone at the graveside, alongside a few of Abe's workers. No one spoke.

They began to disperse, but Niblett came over to him. 'Hal Mannory?' he said. 'I'd be obliged if you would come to my office.'

Whatever next, Hal thought, and why me?

Niblett sat him down on the far side of his impressive desk. He opened a drawer and pulled out a folded piece of parchment, which he proceeded to open somewhat ceremoniously on the desk.

'You are Hal, son of Judith Fuller, known by the surname Mannory and lately Attfield?'

'Er, yes,' Hal said.

'I am required to read to you the last Will and Testament of Abraham Trussler of Tanfield in the Borough of Farnham.' He looked over his spectacles to make sure Hal was listening. Despite his bewilderment, Hal was certainly listening.

Niblett referred back to the document. 'The usual pious preliminaries,' he said. 'Then it continues "I give my tannery known as Tanfield with the messuage thereon to Hal, son of Judith Fuller, known as Mannory and lately as Attfield, together with my dwellings in Abbey Street, and I bequeath to him all the tools of my trade, my horse, my cart, my bed, my table",' Niblett broke off. 'These are listed along with a number of domestic items. I'll not go through the list now, the rest are of no great consequence.'

He took off his spectacles and looked earnestly at Hal. 'What age are you?' he asked

'About seventeen,' Hal said.

'You will need a fiduciary,' Niblett said.

'A what?'

'A fiduciary. A trusted grown man whom I as executor will appoint to act for you, to look after the inheritance, until you come of age at 18 years.'

'Oh. Yes.' Hal said.

'Tanner Mannory perhaps?' He folded up the parchment. 'As soon as the Will has been proved, that is to say granted probate by the Court, you will be a man of property. I congratulate you,' and he stood up and shook Hal's hand.

Hal was dumbstruck. Niblett had one or two more points of business to tell him which he barely heard. He left the office and walked slowly to the Attfields' house, one thought insistently with him.

He stood stiffly inside the door, watching Ralph and Abigail at work, yet scarcely seeing them.

'I went to the funeral,' he said.

'Abe Trussler laid to rest at last,' Ralph said, still plying his needle.

'Attorney Niblett took me to his office.'

They looked up, questioning.

'Trussler has left all his property, tannery and everything,' he gulped, 'to me!'

Exclamations of astonishment slid over him, as he struggled with tears. It was all he could do, to explain.

'Abe once claimed,' he said, 'that he might be my father. Because he often had my mother in lieu of rent.' He paused.

'If this bequest means he was my father...' he broke off as his eyes filled with tears. 'I don't want him to have been my father.'

Ralph slowly put aside the harness he was making. He stood up and went to Hal. He put an arm round his shoulders and led him to a bench, where he sat beside him, still holding him.

'Family likenesses speak loudly,' he said quietly. 'Do you remember that time during the war when the cavalry horses were quartered at the Tanyard? You helped move them, and Jim Hosier thought you were Thomas' brother. You and Thomas look remarkably alike.'

'And Hal,' Charity said, 'Walter Hutchcroft recognised me because for a moment he thought I was my mother. Family likeness. I'm sure you are a Mannory.'

'In fact,' Ralph said, 'Long ago, before I married Abigail,

Jacob Mannory told me that he considered himself to have fathered you. You resemble him as well.'

'So Abe wasn't my father?' Hal sniffed. 'Then why has he left me all this?'

'Maybe you were one of the few who were civil to him? And what was that wheel incident everyone talked about?'

'If that was all, it's a huge return.' Hal wiped his eyes on his sleeve, and smiled. 'What on earth am I to do with so much property?' he said.

Hal wanted all in their close group to hear the news as soon as Thomas was next in Farnham, before it could become public knowledge.

'Attorney Niblett says I'll need a fed…iduciary, until I come of age,' he told them. 'Someone Mr Niblett approves, and then once the will is proved we can use the inheritance as we wish. So long, that is, that we consult him. And he'll hold any rent or profit until I turn eighteen.'

'Who will be your fiduciary?' Ralph asked.

'Niblett suggested Tanner Mannory, but Ralph, would you be willing to be that for me?'

'With you rather than for you,' Ralph said.

Thomas was hardly listening. Then he said, 'I wish I had made my peace with Abe before he died.'

'Oh Tom.' Abigail looked at him sadly. 'Peaceable brother, and just one relationship where you were not at peace.'

'Too late now,' Thomas said. 'I really hated him.'

'We're not supposed to pray for the dead,' Abigail said, 'like the Papists do. But you'd think something could be arranged in heaven if you really want to make peace with him.'

'If he's in heaven,' Thomas muttered.

'Best leave that judgment to God,' Ralph said.

Hal's first priority was to visit Tanfield. He found little going on. Two men were moving suspended hides from one pit to another, while a third, he with whom he had spoken before, seemed to be vaguely supervising. He looked up as Hal walked into the yard.

'Here comes the new master,' he called to the others in mocking tones.

Hal shook hands with him. 'I'm not even the owner yet,' he said, 'not until the court has approved the will.'

He started to talk tanning. Not for nothing had he lived four childhood years in the Mannory tanyard, menially employed but with eyes always open. The men were clearly surprised at his questions and observations.

'So do you intend to run this tannery?' the supervising man said.

'I don't know what I shall do yet,' Hal said, 'but I'll make sure you are all paid. No point in running down a going concern.'

The man looked him up and down. 'It was you who brought that wheel, wasn't it?' he said. 'And you called in one day when he was sick.'

Hal nodded. Then he said 'The horse that Master Trussler had. Is it still here?'

'The old nag? Not up to much. Hardly been worked lately.'

'I'd like to take her if I may. She could graze with our three.'

Ralph laughed when Hal told him. 'The first thing you do is acquire a horse!'

'Have you heard?' James was hardly through the door when Ann assailed him. 'Have you heard about Abe Trussler?'

James, deep in his own thoughts, shook his head.

'About Abe Trussler's bequest,' Ann said. 'You'd never guess! He has left all he owned to Hal!'

'To Hal? But he's nobody.'

'Not nobody any more! And he not yet twenty! And James, just think! He's inheriting Trussler's tannery. Tanfield isn't it?'

'He's no tanner,' James said. 'He never got beyond shredding oak bark for tannin before he went off to be with the Army horses.'

'But James!' Ann could not contain her excitement. 'You could take over that tannery.'

James sat down. But Ann had not finished.

'I was going to tell you, and then I heard about Tanfield, but I'll tell you now. Word got about that I sew well, and now I'm to be dressmaker to Mistress Vernon, at Culver Hall, sewing for her and her daughters. So it won't be just my hens bringing us in some money.'

James looked at her dumbly.

Am I to be dependent on my wife?

Am I to be subject to a bastard assistant carter? Why, I used to beat him as a boy when he was slow to obey.

How low can a man be brought?

Yet Ann was waiting for him to respond, to share her excitement, excitement which was rapidly ebbing from her face. He had reluctantly to admit that he was surprised at her enterprise, surprised too that she had actually kept her promise not to gossip about their situation.

'So it has come to this,' he said. 'At least some good has

come of the gossiping.' Then seeing her dejected expression he stood up

'Much to think about,' he said, and kissed her.

Talking with seamen in Southampton kept Thomas in touch with what was happening along the coast. At the end of August the two hostile fleets had sighted each other, but bad weather prevented them from engaging in fight. The royalist fleet returned to Helvoetsluis. The Earl of Warwick's fleet soon followed and blockaded them in.

For two months Kiffin and his fellow merchants could therefore trade in safety. But by the end of November, reluctant to allow his fleet to winter in those shallow coastal waters, Warwick ordered it back to the Downs. Prince Rupert, renowned as a General and now appointed Admiral of Prince Charles' fleet, took advantage of the move. Sailing down the English Channel towards the south of Ireland, he took prizes as he went.

'I see no logic in war,' William said. 'Prince Charles sends out to capture merchantmen, calling them prizes to finance his fleet, and threatens the sea trade of his father's kingdom. Trade is the kingdom's wealth.'

'If King Charles is being held as a prisoner on the Isle of Wight,' Hanna said, 'Does he still have a kingdom?'

'He's still King in title,' William said. 'He waged war against his subjects and his Parliament, and now this. It's his people who suffer.'

In London, opinion swung wildly on every aspect of the kingship and of Charles as King. Cromwell was one whose attitude hardened as time went on, saying that no solution seemed possible while the King remained alive. Lilburne on the other hand became convinced that the King as ruler would be preferable to Cromwell. Meanwhile recurring efforts to have *An Agreement of the People* accepted and put into practice, stalled time and again. And reasonable Rainsborough was dead, either assassinated or the victim of a kidnap attempt which went wrong.

A date was set to re-open negotiations with the King. Starting in mid-September, forty days were to be allowed in which to arrive at a conclusion.

The quayside in Southampton was thronged when Thomas inched his cart towards the berth of the grain ship. John Woodbridge hailed him from the edge of the crowd.

'At last!' he said. 'Parliament has set up the commission, and the commissioners are on their way.'

'There seem to be a lot of them,' Thomas said.

'Four from the House of Lords and six from the Commons, and all their servants and their baggage. Walter in the guise of my servant has made a point of becoming acquainted with some of the servants. A good source of information.'

'It is said that servants know more than their masters credit them with,' Thomas said.

'Well, these commissioners are quite a mixture. Some lawyers as you might expect. Half of them negotiated with the King during the war, so they know what they are up against. They are not all of the same persuasion – Presbyterian, Independent, backing the Army, mistrustful of the Army, in favour of constitutional monarchy, or even a republic, and some of their personal animosities are well known.'

'It sounds as if as chaplain you will be kept busy keeping

the peace among them,' Thomas said.

Woodbridge smiled, but before he could reply a cry of 'John!' from a man emerging from the crowd caught his attention.

'Harry! What joy to see you! After all these years!'

He turned to Thomas. 'Sir Henry Vane, one time governor of Massachusetts.'

'Ten years ago,' Sir Henry said, 'and in trouble then over freedom of conscience. So you are to be chaplain among us, I hear. You will have your work cut out.'

'As will all of you,' Woodbridge said. 'But you, Harry, can be relied upon to bring some wit and humour to the discussions.'

Sir Henry laughed. 'Ultimately the question is very serious. Can there be peace while the King remains king, indeed if he remains alive?'

Woodbridge caught his seriousness. 'All the King's stalling and refusals to compromise are driving some to desperation.'

'But can the removal of problem people ever solve the problems in the long run?' Sir Henry said. 'Removal from the Commons of those of Presbyterian persuasion leaves a small government of Independents, and they cannot agree among themselves. Now that there is peace with the Scots, attention may turn on Lilburne and the Levellers, who as you say are becoming desperate. Getting rid of them will only shelve the reforms they have promoted. Driving out those who oppose you doesn't solve problems at any depth.'

'Do you have any hope for these new negotiations?' Woodbridge asked.

'Compromise is all we can hope for. I would like to see a constitutional monarchy, and no state church. We'll have to reach some conclusion to report back to Parliament.'

He smiled again and took Woodbridge's arm. 'Enough. Tell me how you fare yourself, and your family and your fortunes,' and they settled to a brief exchange of friendship, a friendship forged in the short years that Sir Henry had been in Massachusetts and Woodbridge at work in the magistrates' court. Thomas led the horses on through the crowded quay. Frank came fleetingly by.

'New assignment,' he said. 'Escorting the King to Newport every day. Not far, but he could escape on the way.'

'Newport?' Thomas asked.

'Capital of the Island. Parliamentary commissioners trying to negotiate with the King, meet him there.'

As ever, negotiations went back and forth, the King appearing to agree, only subsequently to retract. The forty days ran out and were twice extended.

Chapter 19 - Charity's Choice

'**M**ay I come in?' Charity looked over the half door into the dim stable. Hal had a lamp lit, for the November twilight was drawing in. He looked up and smiled.

'You've never come here before,' he said.

'I wanted to talk with you away from everyone else.' She leant against a stall partition and watched him grooming a little old mare.

'She belonged to Abe Trussler,' he said. 'She's better already for food and care. I put her to the cart last week. Just for a short run with a light load.'

'Do you ever go to Southampton with Thomas?'

'That's his run. I've plenty to do here. Thomas is building up the business. He'll use Abe's cart once the little mare is at full strength, and new carters.'

'And you his partner?' Charity's question was left in the air. 'The gossips are saying that as a man of property you will be a desirable husband for someone.'

'Plotting mothers!' Hal laughed.

'But Hal. Tell me what I should do.'

'I can't do that. I can't make choices for you.'

'Choices are so hard. Just telling you about it may help me. You know Walter Hutchcroft?'

'Your father!'

'My father. He doesn't feel like my father.'

'What is a father meant to feel like?'

'What does Master Mannory mean to you?'

'I don't feel anything particular for Master Mannory. He was always stern with me when I was in his household as a child, as if he regretted fathering me. And I certainly never had any feeling for Abe Trussler, for all his claims of perhaps being my father.'

'The fact of conceiving a child doesn't make a man into a father,' Charity said. 'I mean, a father surely has a certain role. That must have to be built up as the child grows.'

'Ralph has been a father to me,' Hal said.

Charity looked at him thoughtfully. 'Yes,' she said, 'He's a father figure for me too. But as to Walter, I think of him as Walter. To call him "Father" wouldn't come easily.' She giggled. 'The gossips haven't managed to discover that he is my father. They assume he is a lover, come from nowhere.'

She ran her fingers through the horse's mane, suddenly serious. 'At times he is so affectionate that he could be mistaken for a lover. As if he is confusing me with his Martha; bringing her to life again in me. He is delightful and interesting, but sometimes I am wary.'

She watched as Hal spread a horse blanket over the mare, securing it in place.

'Walter,' she said, 'wants to take me to Massachusetts with him. He wants me to be his family, to live as his daughter until he finds me a husband and I give him grandchildren. He says it will foster an adventurous spirit in me.'

'Has he told you what it's like out there, in the place they call Andover?'

'Thick forest beyond their clearings, and all the men are obliged to carry guns. Very hot in summer, very cold in winter. Wild winds from the ocean.'

'It doesn't sound hospitable,' Hal said.

'Walter says the people are hospitable and friendly. He keeps writing letters to me about it. But Hal, it would be starting raw all over again.'

'Like when you came to Farnham?'

'Like when I left the farm. That wasn't a happy place, but it was what I knew. Now Ralph and Abigail and dear Simon have embraced me into their home. They've become as family to me.' She picked a piece of straw off Hal's shoulder. 'In my old life, it was as if decisions, choices, were always made for me, about me. Do I want to be wafted away by someone else's wishes, and have a husband selected for me in a strange place? Walter will be hurt and sad if I refuse to go with him.'

'Ralph and Abigail are sad over my decisions,' Hal said. 'Ralph hoped that I'd become a horse-collar maker and join his business. He tried and tried to get me apprenticed and failed. But he knows my love of horses, and after all it is a love that he shares.'

'Like bringing Abe's horse back to health?'

'More than that. I'm planning to move Petersfield way. An old friend of Ralph's, Jim Hosier, runs a stud there, and I'm to work with him.'

'What did Ralph say about that?'

'He thought long and hard, and then he said, "I have to let you go". I guess that is what fathers have to do for their children. Ralph is a generous man. He gave me his blessing.'

'Not holding on,' Charity said.

She was silent for a while. Then she said, 'What will you do with Tanfield, Abe's tannery?'

'That question has been answered for me. James sought me

out to ask if he might rent Tanfield from me. He said he can't afford to buy it but would pay rent. It must have been hard for him, to ask the brat he used to beat, to be his landlord.'

'He's a proud man. Asking you must have cost him dearly.'

Hal held the door, about to lock up for the night, and Charity moved with him. 'So you are going away, and Ralph is disappointed. And Walter is going away, and he will be disappointed if I don't go with him. I want to make my own decision, and I have to decide quickly, because the ship bringing John Woodbridge's wife and children has been sighted. Once they arrive and are settled, Walter will go back across the ocean to look after their property and affairs. Imagine, two or three months in a ship to get there!'

The last time Thomas saw Frank he was loading a pack horse. 'Colonel Hammond is dismissed as Governor of the Island,' he said. 'We're off to the Army headquarters.'

'And the King?' Thomas asked.

'They're moving him to Hurst Castle off the mainland. Bleak place. One of old King Henry's forts.'

'What about those discussions he was having?' Thomas asked.

'At Newport? Finished. Parliamentary commissioners gone back to London.' Frank tightened a strap on the horse's saddlebag. 'Parliament rejected it. Treaty of Newport annulled. Waste of time. Game of chess. I'll stick to what I know.'

Colonel Hammond's successor caught up with him in Farnham. There he had him arrested as too sympathetic to royalists, and escorted to the Army grandees at Windsor.

Far more memorable was the day King Charles himself passed through the town.

The King was brought from Southampton in stages, spending the first night at Winchester. Colonel Harrison, a courteous gentleman for all that he was an ardent Independent who advocated a republic, had charge of a relief escort which was to take over duties at Bentley. Early in the morning of 19th December he roused the Farnham Burgesses to order wood and candles, tobacco and pipes, to be delivered to Culver Hall, where he alerted the Vernon family that they were to host the royal visitor.

Word spread fast. Along the way little knots of people gathered to catch sight of the King, to bless him as he rode by, to perhaps receive the mythical royal healing touch. More and more of the townsfolk assembled outside Culver Hall.

Seeing the eager look on Charity's face, Abigail said, 'You go along if you wish.'

Charity wrapped one shawl round her head and another over her shoulders, and stood on the edge of the crowd standing opposite the house. Little could be seen of the King's person as he rode into the Culver Hall stable yard, where Master Vernon greeted him. Not satisfied with such a poor glimpse, people began to follow into the house itself where they could gape at the King as he supped.

'You're well disguised under those shawls!' Charity turned towards a familiar voice. It was Thomas. 'Do you want to go inside?' he said.

'It's their private house,' she said. 'I don't know that I'd like to go inside.'

'The King must have a strange life,' Thomas said. 'I mean he's a closely guarded prisoner, defeated in war. And then people want to honour him because he's King. Or maybe they just want to see what a King looks like.'

'Fancy having to eat your supper with an audience!' Charity said.

'Seen enough?' Thomas said.

They started to walk back along West Street, into the cold wind.

'So we're to lose Hal,' he said as they walked, 'my faithful carting assistant, off to a stud farm. Will you miss him?'

'Yes I shall,' Charity said. 'He's like a brother to me, at least what I imagine a brother would be to his sister.'

'Not a sweetheart?' almost a question.

'A good friend,' Charity said. 'He helps me to understand.'

'And Walter Hutchcroft?'

'Gone back to Massachusetts.'

'And you not with him?' Thomas sounded incredulous.

All that Charity said was, 'No.' Then in fairness she added 'That is what I chose.'

There was a kind of privacy, walking away from the crowd whose focus was in the other direction. Each looking straight ahead as they walked, there was a kind of privacy from each other too. An odd place to speak his heart, yet to Thomas it seemed an opportunity to be grasped.

'You remember when Ann betrayed your confidence?' he said. 'When she suggested that I'd fought that rapist because I desired you for myself?'

'Until Ann said that, I'd always thought that you fought him out of pity for me. But then Ann did make me wonder,' Charity said.

'That was true at the time,' Thomas said. 'I fought him because I thought him a blackguard, and he threatened to kill you.' They were nearing the house now, and soon he would

245

have to let her go in. They stood still, by Wroth the linen draper's shop, and he turned to her.

'But Charity,' he said, 'now that I've come to know you, to value you,' he paused. 'I do desire you for myself.'

Charity did not answer directly. 'I've tried,' she said, looking down the faintly discernible street: 'I've tried to forgive that soldier and what he did to me. Because of what we've learnt. But it's hard.'

'Forgiveness is costly,' Thomas said. 'It cost Jesus his life.'

He touched her shoulders and turned her to face him. 'Would you have me?' he said.

'Will it hurt?' Charity said.

Thomas gave a little laugh, standing there in the dark. 'Is that your "yes"?' Then he said 'I'd always try to be gentle with you. You deserve that.'

She moved towards him and allowed him to wrap his coat, and himself, round her shivering body. 'I love you, Tom,' she said.

In the morning they watched as King Charles rode off to his trial and death.

The End

Afterwards

The Commonwealth years brought no encouragement to those who had campaigned for justice and reform. Habeas corpus, making it possible to appeal against unjust imprisonment, was codified in 1679, but 200 years and more passed before matters such as jail fees, prison for debt, education etc. were gradually addressed, universal manhood suffrage being enacted only in 1919.

John Lilburne and his pen were seldom idle, with episodes in prison and even exile, although he remained enormously popular. He died, still quarrelsome and worn out at 42, in 1657.

Richard Overton had a similar history, although he unlike Liburne was prepared to compromise, and may even have acted as a double agent.

John Wildman also wrote, and plotted throughout his life.

William and Hanna Kiffin had several children from 1649 onwards. Lydia, known as Hanna after her mother, married Ben Hewling in her teens. William lived until 1701, a staunch support for Nonconformists, weathering the Restoration of the monarchy and personal tragedy.

The Levellers, fragmented through war in Ireland and internal disunity, received a final blow when mutineers were crushed at Burford in Oxfordshire in one of Cromwell's lightning strikes.

John Woodbridge succeeded in publishing Anne Bradstreet's poems in 1650, without her permission. Dismayed that she had neither approved nor had the chance to edit and correct, she was won over by their immediate popularity. John and his family remained in England until returning to Massachusetts in 1662.

Mannorys (or Manwarings) continued as Farnham tanners well into the 19th century.

Attfields were harness makers and saddlers into the 18th century.

Christopher and Joan Gary are recorded as having just the one daughter, Jane.

The Vernon family continued at Culver Hall, now known as Vernon House.